A PROSPECTOR'S DREAM

******

MANUELA SCHNEIDER

WOLFPACK
PUBLISHING
— EST 2013 —

Paperback Edition
Copyright © 2021 (As Revised) Manuela Schneider

Wolfpack Publishing
6032 Wheat Penny Avenue
Las Vegas, NV 89122

wolfpackpublishing.com

Paperback ISBN 978-1-64734-993-6
eBook ISBN 978-1-64734-992-9

A PROSPECTOR'S DREAM

* * * * * *

ACKNOWLEDGEMENTS

***

I want to thank the following people for making this book possible:

My wonderful editor Denise F. McAllister. Not only has she done a wonderful job editing my books but also blessed me with great advice and expertise. I have learned tons about writing since working with her.

My publicist Krista Rolfzen Soukup of Blue Cottage agency who has designed a new path of following my dream for me.

Bestselling author Harlan Hague, who has helped me tremendously on my way to self-publishing. He never tired of answering my numerous emails and found inspiring people for me to work with.

And last, but not least, I thank the amazing town of Tombstone that never fails to inspire me. Walking down famous Allen Street is a trip back in time.

CHAPTER ONE

***

At long last, he was in Arizona—the dusty, yet promising land of the silver and gold boom prospectors. After weeks of the strenuous thirteen-hundred-mile journey from Turner, Kansas across the forests of Colorado and parts of the Southwestern territory to the hot Sonoran Desert, Jesse Connor finally reined up his horse-drawn wagon. He relaxed for a few minutes and surveyed the old adobe ranch house that would be his home.

Jesse considered himself more than lucky to have made it to Cochise County without getting killed by road agents or renegade Indians. The journey had been tough, and he was as exhausted as the two horses pulling his covered wagon. Jesse climbed down and stretched his stiff back, wincing as he felt pain stabbing his spine.

"Lord, I can't recall ever having felt this worn out. Dang, every single bone hurts. Didn't even know all the places that can hurt in a body."

He gazed around his property. The small house sure looked as if it needed some repairs. The crude, damaged door hung sadly in its weathered frame, and the stucco had chipped off the walls in spots. Nevertheless, it was his own. With the right tools and building materials he would soon convert it into a real home. Right now, however, the Adobe house didn't look welcoming at all.

Jesse hoped that the roof didn't leak. Fortunately, he had the money from the sale of his tiny farm in Kansas and had been willing to take the risk of reinvesting it in Apache territory.

Accustomed to hard work, the young lad was sure that the small building would eventually become a cozy love nest for him and his beloved wife, Maggie. Of course, he wasn't naïve and knew that more than a handful of work awaited him here. Jesse had set his mind on prospecting mines like so many others in the territory. It was back-breaking labor—at least folks had told him so.

At the moment he was relieved that Maggie was back in Kansas with her family for the time being. Not that Jesse didn't feel lonely, for he surely missed her company.

It was a demanding task to travel cross-country all alone, and it was mighty dangerous, too. But despite that, he had decided to settle first and get the house ready for his wife. The young fellow wanted to fashion their living quarters as to be welcoming as possible since Maggie had become a steady complainer lately, or had she been from the start?

She obviously hadn't approved of the idea of moving away from her parents' hometown. Neither did she appreciate his plan to try for a lucky strike in the desert territory. And when Maggie was upset about something, she didn't hold back—instead, she expressed her opinion loud and clear. She had been quite standoffish the weeks before Jesse hit the trail and sometimes seemed madder at him than an old, wet hen.

Maggie came from a well-to-do ranching family, and she treasured all the amenities that money could buy. He could understand her doubts about moving out West. But who said that she wouldn't be able to afford to buy whatever she liked if he struck pay dirt?

Travelling out here by himself had provided plenty time to review their marriage and its development since getting hitched. Jesse would be lying if he said that he was happy with the course of their relationship the past few months.

So far, they hadn't been blessed with children. He wondered if she had tried to prevent a pregnancy. Jesse knew there were ways to do so. The soiled doves in the bordellos used all kind of tricks to avoid having children, not knowing who the father might be.

He sure would love to hear the cheerful laughter of a youngster welcoming him home from working in the fields. It gave a man a reason to work hard, knowing that his achievements helped create a better future for his family. "Well, maybe it will happen here in Tombstone," he mumbled while unhitching his horses.

Jesse was aware that, as a simple, but hardworking fellow, he was far from Maggie's parents' dream son-in-law. They would have rather their daughter married a salesman or banker or maybe a cattle baron with a big ranch in Kansas. Their offspring had been spoiled since childhood, and sometimes Jesse had the definite feeling that she had married him on a whim, not out of love. She didn't seem willing to share his dreams or sacrifice certain luxuries to support him. Sometimes he wondered if she believed in him as a man, or in their future together. They didn't seem to pull on the same rope.

Jesse was aware that Arizona was a dangerous territory full of outlaws, hostile Indians, and snakes, to name but a few predators. The climate was scorching during summers, with monsoon storms that often triggered fever among the pioneers, but he had heard and read enough to be convinced that he could actually make a fortune in the mines of the territory.

Maggie might not like it in Tombstone but she would endure it, if he struck it big and made enough money to pamper her. And that was indeed his intention. *It's about time to prove that I'm worth as much as a dang banker.*

The tired man shook off these unpleasant thoughts and unloaded the wagon. By the time he was done he was covered in sweat and dust. It was early spring, but the daytime temperature was already quite warm. *How hot will summers get?*

Jesse tried to form a clearer picture of the damage in and around the house to figure out what he needed to pick up at the Tombstone Mercantile the next day. He would definitely need some nails, wood boards, bricks, a wheelbarrow, and likely even more.

A lot of scrub and cacti would have to be cleared around the property. But the young man had already decided to keep the larger mesquite trees for the sake of the cooling shade they provided. Maybe he could build a small bench for Maggie to sit under one of the trees in the evening after the day's chores were done. *She would surely love that*, he thought.

The adobe structure felt pleasantly cool inside and kept the early spring heat out. He hoped it would retain the warmth of a burning fire inside the walls during cool winter nights as well.

Since the mattress of old, rotten straw didn't look promising, Jesse tossed it out of the house and slept on the floor with his saddle as a headrest. It would do for the first night as he was exhausted enough to sleep in a dried-out wash. Tomorrow things would look much better once he got some tools and maybe a clean sack of straw and a new blanket as well.

Surprisingly it had cooled off pretty quickly and felt chilly now. He listened to the howl of the coyotes for a few minutes, but gave in to weariness and slept dreamlessly.

CHAPTER TWO

***

A few miles down the trail from Jesse Connor's new home, the town of Tombstone was bustling and noisy. Its nightly entertainment was well-known throughout the West.

Allen Street was crowded. Tombstone featured a large number of saloons which resulted in hundreds of shady ladies roaming the streets and standing before brothels in search of men willing to pay for their favors. The nights in the boomtown were loud and rough, and whiskey flowed freely from the oak barrels twenty-four hours a day, seven days a week.

Lorraine Bernard was one of the most successful ladies of ill repute in Tombstone and was in the enviable position of being able to select her customers. She decided to whom she would grant the passion of her body to, and to whom not. She didn't have to follow orders from anybody.

Of French and English heritage and exceptionally beautiful, this particular fallen angel indeed appeared most heavenly. Like other girls, she had arrived in Tombstone as a showgirl with a traveling circus, but soon realized there were much better business opportunities here and stayed.

The circus wandered farther westward toward California to perform in other towns caught up in the fever of the gold and silver rush.

Fortunately, Lorraine had never been in the same depressing situation as the poor girls down on Toughnut Street or Sixth Street. They had to sell their bodies in dirty cribs which were nothing better than a tiny, sparsely furnished wood shack where they slept after the men left. Some girls sold their bodies in tents.

Lorraine met such a lost soul a few days ago and had exchanged friendly words with the pale woman. "Have I ever seen you before? You look tired, and you seem to have a fever. Why don't you try to rest a while?"

But the soiled dove shook her head, while trying to suppress a bad cough. She must have been in her late thirties.

"I can't rest. I just got here a few days ago from Benson. My husband got shot in a poker game, but not before the fool lost our farm to the dang cards. I had to leave the house and have nowhere else to go. So selling my body is the only way I can feed my little girl. She stays with me in the crib."

Lorraine pitied the woman. She had seen countless life stories like that, so she gave the widow an extra dollar to get a decent meal for her child.

Lorraine had never faced that hardship as she was blessed with a rare beauty. She was highly educated and charming as well. As this was a rare combination along the frontier where women were generally outnumbered by men, Lorraine was immediately hired at the Oriental Saloon and easily made over a hundred and fifty dollars per week. This was a thundering amount when one considered that a miner often earned as little as five dollars per week for his back-breaking, twelve-hour shifts.

"Lorraine, come on over," the guy at the poker table yelled.

The dark-haired woman strolled over to the round table, aware of the countless men staring at her.

"What do you want, Wild Linc?" she asked.

"Well, I was lucky tonight and won some extra money. I want to spend the night with you, of course!"

The others at the table laughed.

Lorraine looked at him through her dreamy eyes framed by fans of long, dark lashes and nodded. Wild Lincoln Duncan had become a regular in her little chamber close to the saloon's bar.

Of Canadian heritage, he was handsome and took good care of his body, unlike the others who had paunches and looked slovenly. The man also knew how to please her. So far it had been easy to fulfill the task of earning money in his arms.

Lorraine walked ahead to the small door of the chamber she rented at the well-known premises. Lincoln Duncan, known as Wild Linc in town, emptied his glass of cheap whiskey in one swig and rushed to follow her.

He would never admit it, but Lorraine had touched his heart more than any other painted cat in the West. And for dang sure, he knew a lot of them. But there was something about her that seemed almost unreal and mysterious.

Nobody knew what was going on behind those dark-green, almond-shaped eyes of hers. They sure were mesmerizing. She was a strong, proud person who provoked men like Wild Linc to try to tame her.

Long, dark hair with highlights of burgundy fell in luxurious waves over her shoulders. A trim figure with curves where men preferred them finished off the package.

Many men in Tombstone wanted to possess her, and quite a few had proposed. So far, she had turned each offer down, although it would be a desirable way out of prostitution. Most of the women of easy virtue would have jumped at such an offer from a decent man. But not Lorraine.

Rumor had it that she'd saved a lot of money, enough to live the life of an honorable woman even without a husband. She was smart and people said that she held shares in one of the mines out of town. What an outrageous thought, a woman owning mining shares! But then one never really knew what Lorraine Bernard was all about.

***

The semi-dark room flickered with the light of an oil lamp. An iron-frame bed appeared almost too small for Wild Linc's extra-tall size. She stood in front of a small wardrobe filled with some of her elegant dresses and unlaced her bodice, a trace of her perfume drifting through the room. Wild Linc felt his passion rising, and he quickly helped her out of her corset, He lay his hands on her, touching her feverishly.

Her natural way of answering his desire never failed to surprise him. It seemed as if she enjoyed the physical contact, which was unusual among the women along the frontier, or should he say among women in general?

When he finally let go of her creamy limbs, he had satisfied his hunger for her body more than once. Lorraine quietly washed herself at the bowl of water on the bureau and got dressed again. He lamented having to leave her, and thought to himself, *I got to ask her if she wants to become my wife*. Linc wasn't a humble feller when it came to sharing things he liked. The frown on his face made it obvious that the many men swarming around her like bees annoyed him more with each passing week.

Duncan put the silver dollars next to her water pitcher, opened the door, and stepped out of Lorraine's chamber.

Immediately the noise of the dancehall girls, the gamblers, and rowdy guests swallowed him. The fallen angel stayed in the room a little while longer, hiding the money in the small pouch she carried under her dress.

I don't feel anything, no disgust, no desire, and no regret. She did what she had to do and was smart enough to play her cards well. As long as she was gifted with charms, Lorraine used her looks efficiently like most of the calico queens in town.

An hour later the dark-haired beauty left the Oriental and walked through a starlit night to the small yet pretty house she called her own. She always carried a small derringer hidden in her dress, and she would not hesitate to use it if any man tried to force himself on her without paying, and, even more so, without her consent.

She was the one in charge, selecting her customers carefully. She received an exorbitant price for her services. Yes, Lorraine Bernard was the most exclusive Hell's Belle in town and she was known for protecting her money almost as securely as her heart.

CHAPTER THREE

***

Jesse awoke tired and not in the best mood. Since he didn't have anything to cook for a decent meal, he decided to go into town, eat and then buy all the supplies needed to set up the house. He wanted his wife to follow him out here to the Arizona territory as soon as possible so the house and property had to be ready.

He saddled one of his horses and rode into Tombstone, which was buzzing with activity. "Gee, it's big! So many buildings," he muttered.

Hunger was foremost in his mind and stomach, so first he visited one of the food shacks, where he enjoyed a hearty breakfast of crispy bacon and eggs and a few cups of strong, steaming coffee. With a full belly, he felt much livelier and stopped at the local hardware and dry goods stores. He had lots of shopping to do for everything he needed—tools, wood boards, a new straw mattress, and firewood. There were no good trees for wood for the stove on his land. With each passing minute, more was added to his list.

While the shop owner gathered everything on Jesse's list, a beautiful woman entered the store. Her dark hair piled up in fancy curls and a dark green, shiny dress hugged her curvy figure.

Two other women in the store whispered behind their hands and looked her over from head to toe. Their expressions were unfriendly, and their mouths showed a bitter downturned line. The dark-haired lady, however, lit up the room with her dazzling smile and didn't pay any attention to the two old hags.

When Jesse completed his purchases, he packed some of the items into his dusty saddle bags, promising the shop owner that he would pick up the rest with his wagon later in the afternoon.

As he left the store, he passed Lorraine standing next to the entrance, deciding about canned peaches. He could see that she didn't care about the gossiping women behind her. Jesse tipped his hat in respect and greeted her with a husky, "Ma'am!" She nodded slightly and their eyes met for a brief moment.

Her face was a pleasant one. *Oh, what a beautiful lady,* Jesse thought. *Well, you got tons of work to do, and no time to stare at the townswomen.* Jesse turned and left.

Lorraine paid for her things and watched the stranger ride out of town. She hadn't seen him before.

"I guess sooner or later he might cross my path again," she whispered.

Jesse kept busy all afternoon. After picking up the rest of his purchases at the merchant, he took care of the leaking roof. Then he fed the two horses and prepared a small meal of dried beef and beans.

While he ate alone, he mumbled "I am wondering how Maggie is doing back with her folks. Well, I reckon it's more peaceful to fix this house by myself. She'd most likely complain about everything until the house is in a more decent state." He chuckled at that thought, imagining her brows drawn together in disapproval, and the corners of her mouth slanting downwards.

Maggie was hard to satisfy. Her parents had spoiled her rotten, and Jesse found it difficult to meet her expectations. Sometimes he wondered why he had decided to settle for her.

Jesse wasn't at all aware of how handsome he appeared to other women. If he had, he might've tried to court someone else instead of Maggie. Someone who would have shared his dreams more enthusiastically.

Jesse was capable of performing almost every job from cowboy to woodchopper and now, as he planned, the labor of a miner. His body was evidence of the hard work he was used to, lean and packed with muscles. Long legs gave him a confident stride, and his dark-brown hair was wavy, thick, and touched his broad shoulders. Yes, Jesse was a good-looking man.

After taking a wash at the pond next to the house, Jesse fell asleep on his new straw-filled mattress. Strangely, the eyes of the beautiful woman he had seen in the store haunted his dreams after he fell into an exhausted slumber.

***

Lorraine was back at the Oriental Saloon. Tonight, she wasn't interested in any of the men offering her their hard-earned money in return for a bit of female tenderness. She sang a tune or two, entertaining the guests who came for a cool drink at the bar or a game of poker.

Like most saloons, the Oriental was well-frequented. It ran twenty-four hours a day, seven days a week, and some guests had a tendency to get violent whenever they looked too deeply into a whiskey bottle. Often those arguments ended in death. There were bar fights every night, and shots were often heard with the screams of the shady ladies who witnessed many of the killings.

Lorraine was one of the regular ladies of the night at the Oriental, but men only succeeded in seeing her naked body if they paid. The other girls would have enough reasons to envy her, and jealousy ruled the territory of the fallen angels in the red-light district.

Although Lorraine was a woman with a determined spirit, she was also a person with a good heart. The other soiled doves liked her for that, despite the competition she posed.

It was an open secret that she had helped quite a few of them out of dangerous situations more than once. Rumor had it that Lorraine stabbed a man to save a woman he was about to choke to death after brutally raping her. There was no proof of the story and the judge would have never sentenced Lorraine anyway. The whole town knew he adored her and was one of the high-ranking customers who paid big money to enjoy her services as a love goddess.

As Lorraine walked home a few hours shy of sunrise, she was lost in thought. She couldn't explain why, but she dwelled on the handsome stranger she met briefly in the store. He greeted her in a friendly and respectful manner. Lorraine was used to men approaching her bluntly, and the contrast of the stranger's kind manners stunned and impressed her.

CHAPTER FOUR

***

Jesse stayed nearby his small house the next few days. It wasn't in the best shape, and it certainly wasn't a mansion, but the repairs were going well. The dwelling looked homier on the inside, and the surrounding grounds more orderly. He intended to create a true love nest and hoped Maggie would be happy and satisfied here.

He couldn't help but have his doubts. *Would she really be comfortable here?* As much as Jesse spurned these thoughts, Maggie often reminded him of a spoiled brat. She was always pretty to look at with her blond hair set perfectly and her beautiful clothes, which were usually costly gifts from her mother. He thought regretfully it was her loving character and commitment to their relationship that was lacking.

Jesse was fully aware he had never been able to give her expensive presents, and it embarrassed him. *If I strike it big, then I'll spoil her rotten and heap presents upon her.* He smiled at that thought. To impress Maggie and make her happy—those were his main motivations for settling in Arizona. He had promised her and was a man of his word.

Got to prove it to myself as well, he thought while replacing another broken shingle on the roof.

That evening Jesse decided it was time to put away his tools and ride into town for a juicy steak and maybe a cold brew. He had worked like a beaver ever since arriving in the new territory and felt he needed a well-deserved break after days of replacing shingles and boards and trying to turn the house into a cozy nest.

After dark, the main street buzzed with people—miners, cowboys, ladies of the night. It seemed like everybody was out roaming the streets. Representatives of all nations wandered around in the Tombstone night: Europeans, Chinese, Black men and women, and even a few of the feared Apaches.

Jesse went to a restaurant and enjoyed a big steak with fresh potatoes. It was a welcomed change from his own cooking, which wasn't fancy at all, and he'd already grown tired of it along the trail. This dinner satisfied his belly, and now he needed to walk it off.

Loud music and laughter rang out from the other side of the street. The board hanging above the entrance of a brightly lit building read the "Birdcage Theatre." Jesse had heard about the place and decided to visit the establishment for a shot of whiskey.

He wasn't a drinker but once in a while a little corn juice couldn't hurt. A nice bar sat to the left, beautifully carved from a massive piece of oak, with wooden pillars supporting the boards that held many tempting bottles. *What an unexpected selection of beverages in this boomtown.* Jesse's mouth fell open a little.

In the back, stairs led to the second level, and he saw girls carrying bottles of alcoholic drinks in willow baskets. Their corsets bared more skin than any decent lady would have ever shown in public. They smiled at Jesse who nodded a brief greeting, without giving them any more attention. He almost laughed at himself. Apparently, he wasn't yet lonely enough to fall for the Scarlet Queens and their charming offers.

Sipping his glass of whiskey, he spotted a stage and small upstairs boxes on both sides—filled with men and the shady ladies who entertained them, swarming around their customers like honey bees.

The upstairs boxes were decorated with painted wallpaper and heavy, red velvet drapes on either side. Jesse noticed that the curtains were closed on some of the niches. Judging by the laughter and male voices that came from behind those drapes, it was clear there was a different sort of entertainment taking place.

"My, oh my, quite a sinful house, I reckon," he mumbled, shaking his head and finishing his whiskey.

Leaving the Birdcage, he heard a piano playing from across the street and a soothing female voice singing one of his favorite songs. He stood on the weathered boardwalk, listening to the tune for a moment.

The music drifted out to the street from the Oriental Saloon, and Jesse decided to stop by and listen to the lovely ballad. He could hardly believe his eyes when he saw the woman he had met at the store earlier in the day. She stood next to the piano, singing. The dark-haired beauty looked gorgeous in an elegant bustle dress of a crimson, satiny material and an embroidered corset emphasizing her slim waist. Her creamy shoulders were bare.

As she sang the sad and haunting Irish ballad, a hush fell over the room. Jesse observed that the men were hypnotized by the singer. When she turned around and saw him standing at the entrance, their eyes locked for the second time.

A smile curled her red lips. He waited until the song ended, joined in the applause, then turned away and ordered another drink at the bar.

"Didn't you like the song?" a throaty, gentle voice asked. Jesse almost choked on his whiskey as he turned to see her standing right next to him.

"Oh, I loved it. But I've got tons of work waiting for me tomorrow, and I'd better not stay up too long. I don't come into town for entertainment."

"Tons of work, hmmm?"

She smiled a dazzling smile. Jesse suddenly felt awkward.

"Well, yes ma'am. I have to repair the house I bought."

"So, you moved here, is it? I guess you plan to jump into the mining business then?"

He nodded eagerly. She ordered a drink for herself and raised her glass.

"To the lucky strike."

He smiled the boyish smile of a rascal and she liked it instantly.

"To the lucky strike," They both took a sip.

"I'm about to leave work for today. Would you mind walking me home?"

He stared at her in surprise and hesitated. She shrugged and turned to go. She was used to being rejected by people.

"Wait, I didn't mean to offend you, Miss."

"Lorraine, Lorraine Bernard, Mister."

"Just Jesse."

"Well then, Just Jesse! I'm not offended. You don't have to worry. I wouldn't try to lure you into an unwanted encounter. So far, men come to see me of their free will," she added with a sarcastic smile.

"Sorry, ma'am, I was just surprised by your request. It would be my pleasure to walk you home, Miss Lorraine."

She retrieved her shawl from behind the bar, and they left together, the glances of a frowning Wild Linc and other astonished men drilling into their backs.

Jesse led his horse along the street as he walked next to the beautiful woman. A trace of her perfume filled the night air. It reminded him of a meadow blooming with spring flowers. Her voice sounded pleasant to his ear. *Hold it, Hoss! Don't forget that you are married and this is a woman of easy morals.*

When they arrived at her house, he tipped his hat and wished her a good night's rest. She nodded. As Jesse turned away, she called him back.

"Jesse, I want to thank you!"

He waved his hand in dismissal. "I just walked you home, no big deal."

"Not for that, Jesse. You called me ma'am at the store, just as you did tonight even after knowing how I earn my living. I want to thank you for showing me some respect. It's a rare thing around here."

He looked at her for a long moment. "Miss Bernard, it's a man's duty to show respect to women."

She smiled.

"Lucky is the woman who enters your life."

He smiled back.

"Tell that to my wife Maggie. She is not so convinced lately … maybe never was," he added bitterly.

With that said, Jesse pulled himself into the saddle, waved goodnight, and left the lady of the night standing in front of her door. She watched him ride out of town, her thoughts lingering on what he had said. When the sound of a horse buggy driving by brought her back to reality, she decided to talk to her partner who ran her mine about Jesse Connor.

CHAPTER FIVE

***

Lorraine Bernard's mining partner was an older fellow called "Cotton Joe," a nickname he had earned thanks to his washed "Long Johns" which always hung over a rope in the backyard of his little cabin. Lorraine had spoken with Cotton Joe weeks prior to meeting Jesse about his needs at the mine. He mentioned he could use someone to help him. *Maybe that feller fits right into the work*, she thought.

The claim was actually hers but she had never made that fact public. Lorraine was smart enough to work in the background, using her business understanding as well as her contacts to achieve the most in life.

Not only did it hold a rich vein of silver, but Cotton Joe struck some gold a few weeks ago, and he believed there was much more in the mine. Their site was only a few miles outside of Tombstone, and didn't compete with the big mines of the major companies. It was a small claim, but well worth prospecting.

***

Jesse Connor arrived back at his adobe house. He'd enjoyed his evening, and his thoughts returned to the woman he walked home.

She didn't fit his idea of a frontier town prostitute, yet that was who she was. Long ago Jesse had sworn to himself not to waste time nor money on such women. Soon Maggie would be following him to Tombstone, so he would endure the loneliness until then.

Lying awake and staring at the ceiling, the young man pondered the mining business. He knew it would be difficult to stake a claim as a newcomer.

Too sparse was his knowledge about prospecting or judging the quality of silver ore. He was also inexperienced when it came to the physically demanding labor of working a mine. The only way for him to get started was to find a mining company to take him on as a hired laborer.

Jesse decided to apply for a job with the "Contention Mine" or "Good Enough Mine" the next day. It was time to turn off his thoughts and get some shut eye.

His full belly, two shots of bottled courage, and all the hard work had worn his body down. He fell into a deep slumber and didn't even hear the coyotes all night.

The following day Jesse went to town early, hoping to catch one of the people who ran the two mines where he'd decided to apply. Perhaps someone could advise him about where to register as a future miner.

He briefly glanced over to the small Victorian house at the end of Toughnut Street where he knew that Miss Lorraine Bernard lived. The house had recently been painted, white with green window frames, and looked charming in the day's sunshine. The flowers in the garden made the home look pretty and welcoming. Jesse couldn't help but wonder if she allowed men to buy her services in her house, or was it her sanctuary?

"Darn, that isn't any of your business," he mumbled under his breath, both annoyed and unsettled by his interest in her.

"So, what is it exactly that is none of your business, Just Jesse?"

Her pleasant voice tinkled like a bell right behind him, and he whirled around, his cheeks growing hot.

There she stood, wearing a smoky grey dress and carrying a big carpetbag purse under her arm. Her hair was braided in a way he had never seen before, resembling a crown. Despite the warm morning sun, she looked as fresh as a spring day.

"Good Morning, Lorraine!"

He didn't answer her question, but she didn't let him off the hook and waited for him to explain himself. He looked down at the tips of his dusty boots and mumbled, "I was wondering if you lived there alone."

He pointed toward her house with his chin. She smiled and sensed he was trying to wiggle out of giving the true answer. Lorraine was better at reading people than others. *Never easy to hide anything from a woman,* Jesse pondered.

"Would you like to join me for breakfast? I just got fresh pastries, biscuits, and coffee."

The question had come out of the blue, and he stared at her, astonished by the offer.

"Actually, I was hoping to catch some mining company folks to talk to them about a job."

He stood before her, hat in hand, nervous like a schoolboy.

"Oh, now that is what I call a coincidence." She laughed. He looked puzzled.

"Well, just so happens that I am looking for a helping hand for my partner Cotton Joe in our little mine down at

Fairbanks about five miles from here. The work is getting to be too much for him to handle alone. In case you are interested, I would be willing to pay you better than the people in the big mines do."

He stared at her in disbelief.

"Wait a minute, are you saying you actually own a mine?"

She gave him an amused look and nodded with a twinkle in her eyes.

"Come on in. Let's talk over breakfast."

She didn't wait for his answer but simply turned and walked toward her house, confident he would follow.

Jesse shook his head, but he followed. He was aware of people who stared at them from the other side of the street and felt a bit uncomfortable about it.

The mysterious shady lady held the door open and invited him into her house. Her home was elegantly furnished, and displayed the taste of an educated, high-class woman. Jesse was deeply impressed and didn't dare sit down on the expensive-looking furniture without being invited to do so.

"I come from a very educated family, Jesse. My father is a successful doctor on the East coast." She frowned slightly. "But none of this has been handed to me. My family turned their backs on me when I started to work for theaters and joined the circus. I earned every single penny to buy all of this, and no, not only through my trade."

Jesse was embarrassed. *Was it really so easy to read my thoughts?* He felt his cheeks heating up again.

"Sit down and make yourself comfortable. I'll brew us some fresh coffee."

Soon afterward the delicious smell of frying eggs mingled with the rich aromas of bacon, and Jesse laughed at the growling sounds that came from his stomach. She offered him a wonderful breakfast, and the coffee was hot and strong, exactly as he liked it.

Fortunately, she joined him for the meal which made him feel less awkward.

"So, what do you think about my offer?" She studied him over the rim of her coffee cup.

He looked at her for a moment and knew it might be risky to work for this astonishing, yet tempting woman. But Jesse had always been a person who liked taking risks, and after all, she offered him a start in one of the mines. So he slowly nodded.

"Same payment as in one of the big mines, you said?"

She nodded. "Jesse, I can afford to pay even better wages compared to the major mines around town, but I must have trustworthy, reliable people around me, for understandable reasons. That's why I selected you."

"You know nothing about me," he objected. "You don't even know my full name, which is Jesse Connor, by the way."

She nodded and reached out her hand to officially introduce herself. "Lorraine Bernard." He shook her hand gently, but her grip was surprisingly strong. She looked at him, a serious expression on her face.

"True that I don't know you, but believe me, I have learned to read people. So, here's my offer. I'll pay you twenty-five dollars per week, which is over seven dollars higher compared to what you would get at the Contention Mine. Plus, I'll hand over a two-percent share of what you dig out of the mine. See it as a kind of success bonus."

Jesse almost choked on his coffee. *Holy cow! That was way beyond the payment I could hope for as a hired miner in Tombstone.* Was this for real or was she bluffing? But then, when he looked around the house, he started to trust her offer. He felt as if she really meant it, and looked as if she could afford to pay him well.

Jesse set down his cup and shook her warm hand once more. "I reckon we have a deal, Miss Bernard."

She smiled and poured him more coffee. Strangely, the fact that she was a lady of easy morals didn't bother him. All he saw was an amazing and beautiful woman who offered him a chance in this town, a chance he desperately needed.

When Jesse left Lorraine's house he was in a cheerful mood. He would earn enough to be able to bring Maggie to Tombstone much sooner than he originally thought.

As he crossed the street, he wasn't aware of Wild Linc Duncan standing in front of one of the opium tents, staring at him.

Wild Linc's eyes glittered dangerously. He turned away, glanced briefly at Lorraine's house, and walked to one of the saloons on Allen Street. When he wasn't in his best mood, he could be a dangerous man. He decided to have a bottle of whiskey instead of breakfast.

CHAPTER SIX

★★★

Lorraine cleared the table. She was satisfied with how the talk about the mining work had gone as she had taken an immediate liking to Jesse Connor. After telling her about the repairs to his house, she figured him to be a hard worker. And he had treated her with respect. So far, he hadn't tried to approach her as a customer, and she really appreciated him for that. Although she had to admit he was quite a handsome fellow—handsome in many ways.

Lorraine left the house to talk to Cotton Joe about her new employee right away and to ensure that Jesse was able to start this week. Money wasn't a problem for her, but she had sensed that he could use a steady income—the sooner, the better for him.

Cotton Joe was just about to leave for the mine after finishing morning chores at his small cabin and getting necessary supplies at the local mercantile. He greeted his approaching boss woman with a friendly smile.

Joe liked her a lot and never saw her as a soiled dove, but rather as his business partner, although she held the larger share. She was smart and beautiful at the same time and a fair partner to run a business with. Much more, Lorraine Bernard had proved to be the most reliable friend a person in this rough town could have. She had actually helped him get away from the deadly grip of the whiskey bottle and given him a chance to start over when nobody else believed in him.

Joe waved at her and waited until she reached him. He always loved to watch her brisk stride. The woman meant business, which was obvious in the way she moved.

"Joe, good morning,."

"Howdy, Lorraine. What a beautiful day, ain't it?"

She nodded in agreement, and they both watched the peaceful blue sky holding a few puffy clouds for a few moments.

"Joe, I wanted to let you know that I hired a helping hand to work with you at the mine. Decent guy, young and hardworking from what I could see of his muscles. His name is Jesse Connor."

Joe winked at her, but she shook her head.

"No, he is not a customer of mine. He's different."

Joe nodded slowly.

"Well, you gave me a chance so I reckon he deserves one, too. Send him to my cabin day after tomorrow. I'll show him the mine and teach him the job. You can count on that. He can start with some digging in the silver shaft. I guess it's in your best interest that I don't show him the gold ore vein yet?"

Lorraine nodded and said, "You got that right. Not yet. We need to get to know him much better before we admit that our simple little mine holds more than silver ready to be chiseled out of its rocky base. As you know, it's all a matter of building trust."

Joe tipped his hat and wished Lorraine a good day. He

didn't say so, but he sure was glad that she had informed him ahead of time about the new hire. He held only twenty percent of the mine, which didn't constitute a controlling interest. She could have hired whomever she wished, but obviously she thought highly of Cotton Joe's opinion despite his past as a notorious drinker. He felt honored that she involved him.

Lorraine never judged people by circumstances, but tried her best to change unpleasant situations in life and believed in the good of people.

Cotton Joe knew that many so-called *respectable* people avoided her because of her profession. He had witnessed the bashing by townswomen often enough.

"Dang fools, you don't even have the slightest clue what a wonderful friend you all are missing out on," he mumbled into his reddish beard.

He knew firsthand how precious Lorraine was, and he would have moved the world for her. Yes, Lorraine Bernard had saved his life, and more than that, she had given him the best life ever after he sobered up. Thanks to her, he had achieved more than he could ever have dreamed of.

Lorraine walked back to her house, small puffs of dust rising behind her shoes under the skirt of her grey dress. She skipped her nightly provision of entertainment and went out for a steak with vegetables in late afternoon instead. Sometimes it felt better to avoid the saloons on Allen Street, including the Oriental. It was an evening off for her simply because she could afford it.

Once in a while Lorraine pampered herself with rare days of solitude in her exquisitely furnished house. She read many books as a way of continuing to increase her education. Lorraine sat absorbed in a book about new mining methods invented in Europe, when she heard the typical noise of rowdy behavior trickling out of the brothels and saloons onto the street. *No, she wouldn't leave the peace of her house tonight, not for all the silver coins in the world.*

A few miles out of town, Jesse Connor lay awake, thinking about the unexpected luck he had encountered today. He had done a lot of work at the house already, and had an incredible job offer which promised more regular income than he could have dreamed of. And even better, he had achieved all that in only the past few days. It seemed as if he was already experiencing his first lucky strike in the town of Tombstone. He prayed that his luck would stay with him for a while.

However, Jesse was a realistic man and knew that a boomtown like Tombstone also drew a lot of thieves, gun-slingers, and outlaws, and he swore to himself to remain alert. He had already seen a few suspicious characters around town.

The next day he needed more supplies from the Mercantile but before going there, he stopped by Lorraine's house. He knocked at the white door and waited. After a few moments, when no one answered the door, he turned to walk to the store. Jesse strolled around the Mercantile and was again surprised at what a variety of different goods it offered, all neatly displayed on the shelves.

After he gathered the necessary items, he selected three apples as well. Jesse had to spend his money carefully and smiled like a child under the Christmas tree as he looked forward to tasting the rare delicacy. It seemed like ages since he had eaten his last ripe apple. He polished one on the front of his shirt and was about to bite into it.

"An apple a day keeps the doctor away."

He would have recognized that melodic voice anywhere. He turned to look straight into Lorraine's lovely face.

After he paid for all of his goods, she ushered him out of the shop and pointed to a small cabin on the other side of the road.

"Cotton Joe, the fellow who runs the mine for me, lives there. I told him about you being a new employee and, if you want, you can start tomorrow. Meet him at that cabin right at first daylight around six-thirty. Joe will take you to the mine and explain everything to you. What do you say?"

His smile grew until it lit up his entire face. "Oh, Lorraine, er, Miss Bernard, how wonderful! I was about to pay you a visit and ask when I could start. That means I can earn my first money right away this week. This is really generous of you. It takes a burden off my shoulders as I had quite a few expenses because of all the supplies I bought so far. Amazing. I really want to thank you."

She smiled back at him.

"No worries. I don't pay you the money for free. The labor is very hard, and I expect a lot from my employees, but I'm also willing to share the gain from the hard work. I wish you a great start tomorrow. Oh, before I forget, I have the food shack deliver lunch out there every day so don't worry about packing food."

He looked at her, baffled, but the beautiful woman simply laughed.

"Well, good food keeps your body strong for the strenuous work so it's in my best interest that you and Cotton Joe eat well. The better shape you are in, the better you'll dig through those tunnels, right?"

"Yes, ma'am!"

She turned and waved goodbye as he bit into one of the delicious apples, grinning like a boy. Now Jesse was indeed happy he had bought them, although it was a treat outside his tight budget.

"How happy the man is about a simple apple," Lorraine mused. Jesse surely was a modest man. She hoped he'd stay that way. The gorgeous lady of the night had seen too many men become spoiled with a rising income.

Greed was one of the diseases that haunted every boomtown in the West, and she had witnessed many lose their lives over it throughout the frontier.

CHAPTER SEVEN

***

While it was still early, Jesse rode home to repair his corral. He had time to build a small shelter for his horses where they could find refuge from the searing summer sun. He always had a big heart for his animals and treated them well.

Working shirtless in the sun, he prepared six forked tree limbs and dug holes into the ground. It was back-breaking to chip through the hard-packed desert soil. The ground was solid clay, and the young lad wondered how hard it must be to dig a mining shaft dozens of feet into the surface.

Once the main support poles were erected, he added a latticed roof that could hold thinner branches. He flattened scrub brush he had harvested from the yard and layered them as a roof. Jesse tied the scrubs to the lattice with twine so his roof wouldn't blow away.

His two horses walked closer to observe what their owner was doing. Jesse's chestnut-colored mare nickered and licked his salty skin. He laughed at the tickle and scratched behind her ears. The gelding wanted his share of petting, too, so Jesse caressed that one as well. Small puffs of dust rose from their dirty coats.

Soon, Jesse turned back to his work, completing everything shortly before sunset. He marveled at the magnificent dusk colors from his small porch while drinking water from an old tin cup. After a wash in the pond, he fed the horses and prepared some hot stew from the left-overs of his previous day's dinner.

"The local food shack delivers lunch to the mine." Lorraine's voice sounded in Jesse's memory, and he shook his head, feeling a deep sense of gratitude.

The handsome adventurer was still worried that he might wake up from this dream, and the vision of a high salary and the supplied lunch would all vanish as quickly as they had appeared.

Jesse lay awake for quite a while, excited about going to the mine the following day. Yes sir, he was ready to start his new job, and he intended to do it as flawlessly as possible. After all, his future and that of his marriage depended on it.

Waking before daylight, he quickly dressed. He munched on a piece of dried beef and a slice of bread while riding to Cotton Joe's cabin. Parts of town were still fast asleep, but Allen Street was buzzing with people and noise, as always.

A commotion caught Jesse's attention. Two fellows were embroiled in an argument, stumbling off the boardwalk in front of one of the saloons and right into the dusty road. It took only a minute until one of them pulled a six-shooter from his holster and plugged his opponent in the gut. It happened in the blink of an eye.

Jesse's horse reared up, spooked by the unexpected noise of the firing gun. It took Jesse a moment to calm the nervous animal, holding tight to its reins and leaning forward in the saddle so as not to be unseated.

A crowd gathered around the body while others shouted and pulled the shooter toward the marshal's office. Now

Jesse understood why Tombstone was known as "The town that takes a man for breakfast." It was easier to get killed here over an argument than over silver. People seemed to prefer drawing their guns to talking things over, and many of the townsfolk appeared to be hot tempered.

Jesse shook his head, disgusted at the puddle of blood on the ground. But he had work to do so he rode to Cotton Joe's cabin where he saw a man standing out front.

Jesse tipped his hat as he got off his horse, holding its reins. "Mister Cotton Joe?"

"That's right, but just skip the mister. It's just Joe. You must be Jesse Connor, right?"

"Yes sir, that's me."

Cotton Joe shook Jesse's hand with a surprisingly strong grip. His body was lean and packed with muscles. Jesse eyed his future foreman. He judged Joe to be in his late fifties with a weathered face and pale blue eyes. His beard and hair were reddish in color, and Jesse assumed he was of Irish origin.

The experienced miner pointed over to the scene of the fight. "What happened? Did you see anything?"

Jesse nodded. "Two guys got into an argument, and one shot the other dead. Guess he thought they'd done enough talking. I think they took the shooter to the marshal's pokey."

Cotton Joe shook his head. "This town gets crazier and nastier with each passing day. Once people get soaked in whiskey or smoke too much opium, they become unpredictable, especially if they've had bad luck mining or gambling. Watch out for them. A life here isn't worth a plug nickel. People don't hesitate for a second to kill a decent man over a ridiculous reason. Doesn't take much, I'm telling you."

Jesse nodded. "I live out of town, fortunately."

"Wise decision." Cotton Joe smiled.

"Well, let's get moving, boy. We'll take the wagon. You can hitch your horse to the tailgate. Takes about half an hour to get out to the mine. Later on, you can leave your mare here in my little corral until we return in the evenings."

Jesse knotted the reins to the wagon's tailgate and climbed on. Cotton Joe whistled to the team of horses, and the wheels rumbled down the road.

"How come people call you Cotton Joe?"

Jesse waited for an answer, and after a pause, Cotton Joe pointed to the backyard of his cabin which they passed that very moment. Long Johns of every possible faded shade between rose and dark red hung over a rope, drying in the morning sun. Jesse laughed a hearty laugh, and Cotton Joe soon joined in. The two men quickly liked each other.

"I hope you agreed with Miss Bernard about hiring me?"

Cotton Joe looked at him. "I have no reason to question her decisions. She knows how to read people. If she believes in you, I do too."

Jesse was surprised at the trust Cotton Joe had in Lorraine's decisions. It was rare that a man believed a woman knew anything about business, especially in a frontier town. Women were meant for other things, like child rearing, school teaching, or saloon work. But in this rough country, pioneer women had to be strong. And oftentimes, men underestimated that strength.

Cotton Joe seemed to sense his co-worker's astonishment.

"Let me tell you something about Miss Bernard. I don't believe in gossip. She's a fine woman despite her profession as a lady of the night. She's smart and knows more about running a successful mine than most fools in this town. Lorraine is hard-headed like a farmer's mule but knows exactly what she's doing. I admire her deeply and no, son, I have never slept with her, neither privately nor as a customer, just in case that question troubles you."

Cotton Joe looked at Jesse intently, and the younger lad besides him blushed like a boy in Sunday School. "I didn't mean to doubt her or be nosy," he apologized but Cotton Joe shook off his objection.

"No harm done, young man. People have no clue who Lorraine really is. You are indeed lucky to have gotten the job. She is very, very picky, and she pays those who are loyal extremely well."

Jesse nodded and told Cotton Joe how surprised he had been about the salary and the job offer.

The two men arrived at the mine. The older prospector pointed at the gate protecting the entrance.

"Jesse, unlock the gate so I can drive the wagon inside the fenced area. We should always close and lock the gate when working underground. You never know who might sneak up on you when you least expect it."

Jesse jumped down from the seat and unlocked the padlock. He stepped aside and waited until the wagon's tailgate passed him, finally closing the gate and locking it from inside. He noticed a shed to the left and a shady Apache-style ramada. To the right he spotted a canvas tent and fire pit.

"The ramada provides shade for the horses and the tent is for us, unless it's too hot, then we can eat under the ramada. It's basic but better than nothing, and, unlike others, we do get a lunch break when food is delivered!"

"Yes, the boss lady told me that, and I couldn't believe it."

"Jesse, she treats me very well, and she'll treat you nice, too. You wait and see. But now it's time to start working. Let's unhitch the horses and I'll show you our tools. Just behind that hill is a small creek where we can water them and refresh ourselves when we need to."

Cotton Joe explained how to best place the candle holder so that it would provide enough light while working underground. Joe handed the hammer and chisel to Jesse and showed him the most efficient way to chisel so that his arm muscles wouldn't become quickly exhausted.

"You won't be able to avoid blisters the first few days, but I have tons of Epsom salt at the cabin to soak your hands in. That will heal them faster than a coyote chasing a rabbit. Once you're used to the work, your hands will grow callouses, and your muscles will get used to the chiseling. This work is really hard on your back, because we spend most of the day in a stooped position underground. You may enjoy a massage down at the Hop Town camp. They can do wonders. China Mary can provide you with anything you wish for down there."

Jesse looked puzzled "Why do you call that part of Tombstone Hop Town?"

"Well, we call it that because of the Chinese population in that part of Tombstone. 'Hops' is a slang words for the opium you can buy there."

Cotton Joe laughed in his hearty Irish way and slapped Jesse on the shoulder. After they had gathered all their tools and baskets, they climbed down a long, wooden ladder into the vertical shaft.

Taking a few careful steps into the darkness lead them to a side shaft which opened horizontally in front of them. Cotton Joe walked ahead. The shaft felt cool considering how warm the morning already was up on the surface.

Cotton Joe pointed to the rear of the tunnel. "This is where you'll start. This one has a nice-sized silver vein. See, you chisel like this!"

While he spoke, he pointed the chisel into the crack

of darker material that showed in contrast to the reddish brown dirt.

Joe loosened a rock the size of a man's fist and held it out to Jesse. It was dark and glimmered slightly, but Jesse never would have made out the silver in it.

The older prospector smiled. "See, once this rock is crushed and the silver ore is extracted, we melt it in big crucibles and pour it into ingot molds. That's called smelting. Of course, some chemicals are needed to purify the silver. Once the process is finished the rock eventually becomes this." He pulled out a silver dollar from his pocket.

Jesse was amazed that it seemed straightforward. Although he was a greenhorn when it came to mining, he was no fool. He understood that painful, endless hours of daily work awaited him, but he was willing to give it a try. Jesse Connor was ambitious and determined to make it in this town. He started his first day of mining with a single burning candle. Cotton Joe's advice about not overdoing the speed but keeping a steady rhythm of well-placed blows of his hammer seemed sound. The chiseling created a plaintive melody of its own in the gloomy semi-darkness.

Time passed so quickly Jesse didn't realize it was time for lunch until Cotton Joe tapped his shoulder, interrupting his work. Joe helped Jesse carry out the baskets of ore. Stepping out of the mining shaft into the bright sunlight momentarily blinded him. He pulled down the scarf covering his mouth to protect his lungs from the dust and gulped in a breath of fresh air.

While he washed his face in the creek, his biceps ached with sharp pain and his hands showed the first raw blisters. But he was still in an optimistic mood.

Cotton Joe looked at him. "Tough work, isn't it? But so far, you're doing quite well considering it's your first day underground. Come on, let's have lunch. You deserve it. The delivery from the food shack arrived. Let's see what Lorraine spoils us with today."

A mouthwatering aroma escaped the tin containers which were filled with meatloaf, mashed potatoes, and freshly baked biscuits.

"I don't believe this. It's a banquet," Jesse mumbled.

"You'd better get used to it. This is the lady's style of treating people as long as you show her honesty and respect."

They both ate in silence. The food was delicious and satisfied Jesse's growling stomach. Cotton Joe got up and poured them each a cup of strong cowboy coffee he had brewed on the campfire. Joe surprised Jesse with sugar.

Jesse enjoyed sitting and resting his arms during the break. The tin coffee cup seemed mighty heavy all of a sudden. He knew he would suffer tremendously from sore muscles for the next two days and hoped he could push through the pain.

Cotton Joe had decided to build up a stronger fire and to break and smelt some of today's ore. It made the time back in the shaft during the afternoon seem shorter. Jesse was well aware that the experienced miner was giving Jesse's exhausted arm muscles a break from chiseling and was thankful for it.

When Joe was finally ready to pour the melted silver into the cast form, Jesse was excited as a child on Christmas morning. The gleaming dark grayish liquid ran over the rim of the crucible, bubbling and roiling. The color reminded Jesse of lead.

"Well, this is today's harvest from the mine."

Young Jesse Connor was aware that Cotton Joe had worked in a different shaft but he would never dare ask how much Joe had gotten out of that mine. He was happy and satisfied to have given his best the first day underground.

"Well, youngster, I think we should call it a day. Let's pack up and head back home."

"Boy, that sounds like great news" Jesse admitted while stifling a yawn.

They hitched the team after washing their faces in the creek. Jesse climbed off the wagon to lock the gate and pulled his tired body back onto the seat. The sun set as they rolled down the hill toward Tombstone.

When they arrived at Cotton Joe's cabin the older man motioned Jesse to wait a moment, then disappeared into the house. He returned with a small cotton sack in his hand.

"Show me your hands, miner!"

Jesse turned his hands palm side up, and Cotton Joe whistled at the sight of all the bloody blisters.

"I expected that. Here's the Epsom salt. Three table-spoons into a bowl of water, soak them well, and bandage your hands. It'll burn and hurt madder than a wasp getting the best of you but the open wounds will close fast. Believe an old miner. I went through the same agony."

Jesse thanked Cotton Joe for all his help and promised to be back the next morning around the same time. When he arrived home, he bathed at the pond, fed his horses, and soaked his hands in the salty water.

It hurt and stung like a thousand needles but eventually his hands felt better. He was too tired to even think about eating and collapsed onto his new straw mattress. He was asleep before he could say his prayers.

CHAPTER EIGHT

* * *

The town buzzed every night, but on miners' payday nightly entertainment venues burst their limits. The Bird-cage Theatre and all the saloons on Allen Street were packed. Hundreds of miners spent their pay on girls of loose morals in cribs around Toughnut Road and Sixth Street. The ladies of the night barely kept up with the men waiting in line for their love services. Some of the prostitutes served dozens of men that night.

The higher-class Scarlet Queens didn't experience such a "rush of traffic." The higher prices in the brothels run by madams kept out the rank and file. And the Oriental was considered a pricey establishment.

Lorraine watched the crowded street through a window. "Isn't it astonishing that so much of the money dug out of the surrounding mine shafts never leaves this town at all?" she whispered to herself.

Lorraine briefly wondered how her new miner Jesse had fared his first day at the backbreaking job in her mine. *Will he return to work the following day?*

But she turned away from the window, shoving her

thoughts about Jesse Connor aside and mingled with the countless male guests.

Her dazzling smile made the pioneers blush at the Oriental Saloon. Lorraine was a queen of the night and no one could distract her from the goals she had set. She pursued them mercilessly. Ignoring her own feelings was one facet of her intense will power.

***

The next morning Jesse woke early. His whole body hurt and his arms felt like the broken wings of an old buzzard. He could barely lift them. "Oh Lord, I wonder if I can hold that hammer at all today," he whined while brewing some coffee. Even so, he whistled a tune in a cheerful mood because he knew the day's work would improve his bank account faster than a dust devil swirling through the desert.

Jesse gazed at his hands and decided to bandage them to protect the raw wounds. He had to grip a hammer and chisel again today.

It was a gorgeous morning, and the sun rose in magnificent colors over the ridge of the Dragoons. Jesse hadn't tired of the awesome sight. Today he was in a hurry to get to town and report to his new boss, so he rode toward Tombstone without contemplating the gorgeous sunrise.

Cotton Joe was outside his cabin and nodded to Jesse. "So you decided to come back?"

"Of course," Jesse laughed. "It's my job, ain't it?"

"You got grit, son. I'll grant you that. Surely you hurt all over, don't you? I see your bandaged hands. Wise decision. I tip my hat in respect. I know quite a few who would've pulled out of this labor by now. It seems you're tough … and loyal. I like that in a man."

"Well, I guess I'm not like some others, then," Jesse

said, getting off his horse. He helped Cotton Joe load the daily firewood and other supplies onto the back of the wagon while he smiled at the famous long johns flapping in the morning breeze.

He briefly glanced at Lorraine's house as they passed by, but focused on his job as they reached the town limits.

He'd learned the important lessons the day before and launched directly into chiseling. It wasn't easy with his sore muscles, and his bleeding hands made it almost impossible to hold the hammer and chisel. He prayed he would have the strength to get through the twelve-hour work shift.

The lunch break was more than welcome, and Jesse looked forward to a warm meal. Cotton Joe brewed some coffee, and Jesse sat on a big boulder near the coffee pot, sighing heavily.

"You look like you could use at least two cups of coffee today so I brewed extra." Cotton Joe smiled. Jesse nodded and smiled back.

Unpacking the mouthwatering lunch, he found grilled chicken and gravy with freshly baked biscuits. Oh, man, what a treat.

Inside another basket Lorraine left a note written in her beautiful handwriting. It read, "For surviving the first hard day underground." Beneath the note snuggled a small apple pie wrapped in a red and white checkered cloth.

"Apple pie? Butter my buns and call me a biscuit! I don't believe this. You'll have to roll me down the shaft after I'm done with all this food."

Jesse took a huge bite of the delicious pie and washed it down with some strong, sweet coffee. Now he felt wonderful despite his aching body. The pie reminded him of his mother's baking, and he felt a twinge of nostalgia. *How I wish she were still alive. I could have brought her to Tombstone along with Maggie.* Sadly, the coughing sickness had killed his mother four years ago, and Jesse still missed her every day.

Cotton Joe gazed at the scenery around them for a moment. Then he said, "When I met Lorraine, I was a terrible drinker. I almost killed myself with that family-wrecking juice. I was homeless, lying in the mud of the street on a rainy day and was about to give up. I wouldn't have given a damn if someone had shot me right then and there. I was literally soaked in whiskey and not able to walk anymore when this beautiful woman came alongside and helped me stand. I must have been a disgusting sight. Nevertheless, she took me to a doctor, who at first refused to even look at me. Son, you should have seen her! She reminded him right away that her services would not be available for him anymore if he didn't help me.

"Next thing I knew, she organized a home and provided me with this job so I could pay off my cabin. Me, a drunk. I mean, I told her she was wasting her time and money. Believe or not, she slapped me right across the face and yelled that I should stop feeling sorry for myself. She told me it was time to act like a grown-up man. Then Lorraine prepared strong coffee and said, 'Sober up, you have a job to do tomorrow!' Yep, that was the way I got to know Lorraine Bernard. You know what she did, son? That woman saved my life. No less than that!"

Cotton Joe's openness about his past touched Jesse's heart. He was deeply impressed when he pictured that pretty woman balancing a drunken stranger on his staggering legs to lead him right into a better life.

Lorraine Bernard was indeed an amazing woman. Jesse wondered how his wife Maggie would have reacted to the sight of a drunk feller lying in the mud. Jesse was quite sure she would have turned away, disgusted.

The afternoon passed quickly despite the long hours of chiseling in the dark, dusty mine shaft. When they were done for the day, Jesse fell asleep on the wagon ride home. He missed the gorgeous sunset and was embarrassed when Cotton Joe woke him in front of his cabin.

The older man just shook his head. "Don't worry, that's normal. As I said, it's tiring work and takes a few weeks to get used to. Don't forget to soak your hands again."

Jesse nodded and mumbled a sleepy, "See you tomorrow." His fatigue and soreness made it hard to pull himself into his own saddle. When he arrived home, he was really beat. He was barely able to finish his chores around the house and tend to the horses. Quickly he crashed onto his straw sack without supper. But he wasn't hungry anyway after all the lunch and pie he had enjoyed earlier.

A smile curled his lips when he thought of the unexpected dessert in the basket. He had eaten better today than the countless weeks before while travelling to Arizona. Exhausted, Jesse fell into a dreamless sleep.

CHAPTER NINE

* * *

Wild Linc enjoyed the company of Blonde Mary, a young French prostitute and madam running a brothel for a well-organized French syndicate in town.

Blonde Mary had a charming accent and was smart enough to run the house of ill repute. Her blond curly hair framed a pleasant face. However, the lush hair didn't hide the slightly bitter expression that often showed on her face.

She was aware that Wild Linc was a regular lover of Lorraine Bernard, so Blonde Mary did everything in her power to lure him into her own arms and away from that Bernard woman.

The French soiled dove had more than a basic female interest in Wild Linc. She was in love with him. She feared Lorraine as unpredictable competition for the blond-haired, handsome man who was well known as a gambler and outlaw in Tombstone.

He was a rough, rude lover, and Blonde Mary often wondered if he sported the same brutal behavior when he was with Lorraine. In Mary's opinion, that dark haired, painted cat was an arrogant snob and probably thought she was better than the other girls serving in the world's oldest profession.

"What gives her the right to think she's higher class than the rest of us?" Blonde Mary whispered to herself with open bitterness in her voice.

Her thoughts were cut short as Wild Linc grasped her roughly by her wrist and yanked her away from the small bar in the entry hall of the poshly furnished brothel. The French knew how to set up a nice establishment, and the women there were charming, clean, and nice to look at.

Wild Linc visited the place often. One could say he was a regular, but none of the women had Lorraine's haunting beauty and skill when it came to fulfilling a man's desires. He only visited Blonde Mary's establishment when he couldn't get time with Lorraine.

The thought of her annoyed Linc Duncan. He had tried to forget her since she hardly appeared at the Oriental lately. The gambler suspected that her absence might have to do with the stranger who moved into town a few weeks back. He'd heard rumors that he worked in the mine she held shares in, if she really owned part of a mine at all.

Wild Linc still had difficulty believing that a woman, specifically a prostitute , would be capable of running any business other than a house of ill repute. But then, people said Lorraine Bernard was a dare devil when it came to living life. And she aroused him as much as she triggered his rage.

The man struggled between falling for her and hating her. Lincoln Duncan was a tough guy and he was used to having things under his control. However, in the case of this exceptional Bernard woman she had always been the one in charge of things, including the control over their liaison, and it was easy for everybody to see that he didn't like that at all.

But he was here now with this curvy French prostitute, and he intended to make the most of the night. Linc didn't care if he pleased her desires, but he wanted his needs satisfied. He was a selfish lover but it was different when he shared the bed with Lorraine. He wanted to give her pleasure and arouse her—even impress her as a lover. The woman lying on the bed next to him now wasn't anything more than a soiled dove he had paid good money for. So he treated her without respect.

Blonde Mary tried to exchange some tenderness, but Linc held her hands down, tore at her clothes, and forced himself on her without paying any attention to her body. He didn't care that he hurt her and grunted like an animal on top of her. As he whispered Lorraine's name when he finally lost control, Blonde Mary heard it. The seed of raging hatred was planted in her heart the very moment his passion swept him away.

When he was finished, Wild Linc got off the bed, dressed in a hurry, and left the room without even looking back at Blonde Mary. If only he had turned around, he might have felt uneasy about the furious mask of pure loathing contorting Mary's pretty features. But in his selfishness, he missed it.

***

Lorraine, of course, knew nothing about that tryst. She was visiting the Birdcage Theatre for a change of pace to watch one of the exotic belly dancers. Nicknamed "Little Egypt," Lorraine had always admired the performer's flexible body. The dancer had taught Lorraine certain moves that could pleasure a man even more.

Wild Linc Duncan was nowhere to be seen tonight and

Lorraine Bernard was thankful for it. The man seemed a bit too attached to her lately, and she wasn't searching for a steady relationship or a husband. She did believe in love, but was too realistic to be naive about it. It was a known fact in town that Lincoln Duncan wasn't the kind of man who would treat a woman with respect. Even though he was usually kind toward Lorraine, she had no doubt he wasn't the type of man a woman should settle with.

***

The days came and went. Jesse got used to the work in the mine. His arms grew stronger as his muscles built up, and his hands healed. His torso showed the results of hard labor. He was even more muscular than when he had first arrived in town.

Cotton Joe gave him his first weekly payment, and Jesse was a bit disappointed that he hadn't received it from Lorraine. The young miner hadn't seen her in many days now. It seemed as if she was avoiding him. *I wonder if she's not satisfied with my work,* he thought after payday.

His first week's wage was more than enough to be able to settle all of his open bills at the mercantile. He had earned over twenty-eight dollars in his first week with the two percent share of the yield, and Cotton Joe seemed happy with his work. Jesse Connor assumed that all was good.

The former farmer had written a letter to his wife Maggie to let her know that he had settled in a nice home. Not only was the house ready for her to move in, but he also worked a good job with a steady income that would feed them both well. His letter didn't hide how much he missed her and that it was time to be reunited as husband and wife.

Now all he had to do was to wait for a letter from her with her approximate arrival date on the weekly stage coach. He planned to buy a nice dressing mirror so she could pamper herself, as a thank you gift for the strenuous journey she would have to face to get to Tombstone.

Fortunately, Maggie would be able to make much of the journey by railway. She could sleep in a Pullman car. Jesse was thrilled that he would be able to bring her to their new home sooner than he had originally expected. Cotton Joe listened to the talk about Jesse's wife and was happy for the young fellow.

The two men had become good friends during their work shifts together. They both knew that one depended on the other when working underground. And both were always aware of the dangers a prospector faced daily.

After receiving his first money, Jesse invited Cotton Joe to the Birdcage to celebrate their friendship and his start in the mining business, but his new friend didn't want to go there. "It is too tempting for me to enter those premises. The smell of whiskey alone is enough to trigger off that demon in me again. I'm afraid."

It was obvious that he was scared to fall back into an old habit, and Jesse understood that well. So, he changed the invitation to one of the finer restaurants in town. To that his partner happily agreed.

The next day both men enjoyed their weekly day off granted by their boss woman. They went to a restaurant with real porcelain plates, fancy tablecloths, and crystal glasses. The two friends felt a bit awkward in the beginning. "I'm sure glad I decided to wear a freshly washed shirt, youngster!"

Jesse laughed and agreed with a smile while he checked the collar of his own cotton shirt. When they saw the menu, they both were as cheerful as little children under a Christmas tree.

The restaurant offered fresh fish brought in on big blocks of ice, a rare delicacy out here in the middle of the Sonoran Desert. The restaurant owner not only assured them of the freshness of the trout but also treated them cordially. He was a "customer" of Lorraine's whenever she would allow it, and of course the restaurant owner knew that these two gentlemen were somehow connected to the beautiful fallen angel he admired so much.

The fish was delicious, baked golden brown in butter, with mashed potatoes and fresh green beans. Cotton Joe relished every bite, celebrating the rare dish. "Man, Jesse, best food I have had in years." Jesse was happy that his friend savored the meal so much. Life was good to him at the moment, and he was grateful.

Both prospectors were just about to enjoy their final cup of coffee out of delicate china cups they could barely hold with their rough, strong hands, when the door opened.

Lorraine entered the restaurant and the conversation around the tables stopped for a brief moment. Jesse couldn't help but to stare at her.

The shady lady looked absolutely stunning. Her hair was pinned up with golden combs and she wore a shimmering dress of dark blue. The candles reflected on the rich material, and her skirt rustled as she walked by.

Jesse saw the older man in her company, respectfully walking two steps behind her. Cotton Joe and Jesse nodded a greeting, and she softly touched Joe's arm.

"Judge Taylor," Cotton Joe whispered.

Jesse nodded. *Yes, Lorraine has sophisticated contacts, no doubt about that*, the young man pondered. The handsome prospector felt underdressed but he managed to shake off the thought. After all, he was her employee, and he didn't need to impress her as a man, or did he?

After a few minutes Lorraine Bernard came over to their table for a moment, greeting both amiably.

"Gentlemen, if you would come by my home tomorrow before work, I'd like to give you last week's pay. Jesse, Cotton Joe told me that he is highly satisfied with your work so far. I hope you have everything you need out there. How is the food delivery? Any complaints or is it still of the same quality?"

Cotton Joe and Jesse both nodded and Joe reassured her that they had all they needed. He explained that Jesse had been so nice to treat him to a delicious baked fish meal in celebration of the first few weeks of working together.

Lorraine smiled her warm, dazzling smile at that news. Then she bid them goodnight and walked over to Judge Taylor's table who quickly jumped up to hold her chair while she sat down.

Jesse stifled a smile at the scene. It was amazing to see men treating the beautiful woman as if she were a highly respected, honorable lady and not a Scarlet Queen. But upon consideration, even he thought she was a lady—at least in certain ways.

CHAPTER TEN

***

Jesse made an effort to follow Cotton Joe's conversation without staring at Lorraine seated across the room. He hadn't seen her in two weeks. *How was it possible that she looked even more beautiful than I last saw her?*

"Jesus, it's really time for my wife to arrive," he mumbled under his breath.

Half an hour later Jesse paid for their food and tipped his hat to Lorraine as they left the restaurant. She nodded, totally professional, and Jesse felt a bit disappointed. Then he cursed himself and mumbled, "What did you expect? You're her employee, dude, *and* you're married anyway."

The two men walked over to Cotton Joe's cabin where Jesse's horse waited patiently. Tombstone became even rowdier and more dangerous once darkness settled over the saloons, opium tents, and brothels. Jesse felt relieved to get out of town.

Yep, it was better to stay in the safety and peaceful loneliness of my little cabin. I just wished I had the warm body of my wife awaiting me there. I'm tired of being alone all the time.

He hoped that their marriage would get better once Maggie arrived to share in his success. *Being away from her interfering mother would probably make things a bit easier as well,* he hoped. Jesse didn't have the heart to admit to himself that Maggie rarely let him touch her. So far, he had denied that his marriage was likely to fail, no matter how hard he tried. But he still believed they had a chance to make it in different surroundings, away from the in-laws.

***

Lorraine spent quite a bit of time at Judge Taylor's house. The man of the bench was a popular bachelor and she knew he intended to ask her to marry him. It was time to tell him that she had no intention of doing so, but Lorraine had to approach it diplomatically. He was one of her most important contacts in this town—a man with power. Judge Taylor could make life easy here in Tombstone, but he could also cause a person trouble.

"Richard, I really appreciate your friendship. But I'm afraid it would damage your reputation and endanger your position as a judge in this town if you married a woman of ill repute."

He shook his head, clearly disagreeing. "We could go to some other town where nobody knows you or your former trade."

She regarded him as if pondering the thought. "Maybe one day that would be possible. However, right now I would rather tend to my business and earn more, so that I can have a so-called honorable life someday."

The judge was one of the few people who knew Lorraine owned a successful mine, and he accepted her excuse immediately. He gently kissed her hand. "I won't give up so easily, my dear. I'm sure some day you'll change your mind." Then he tenderly kissed her cheek and suggested he walk her home.

What Lorraine really liked about this man wasn't only the fact that he was an important person in town, but also that he was a perfect gentleman. Being well off didn't hurt either. He had impeccable manners, came from a highly educated background, and always treated her like a lady. *God knows, there are days when I miss being an honorable woman.* But Lorraine had grown accustomed to suppressing that longing.

She was glad to call it a day. The fallen angel was tired, and seeing Jesse and Cotton Joe at the restaurant had confused her. Lorraine hadn't seen her new employee in over three weeks. It seemed he had developed some new muscles, and the scrub of a three-day-old beard only added to his attractive, rugged appearance. *It took all my self-control to treat them professionally in the company of Judge Taylor. I can't risk the judge becoming suspicious about the new stranger in town.* Lorraine wanted keep people from getting nosy about the mine or her private life and plans. That included Judge Taylor. *But, man, did Jesse look handsome tonight.*

As she undressed, she thought about the next day, and a smile lit up her beautiful face. Cotton Joe and Jesse would come to her house to pick up their pay on their way to the mine. She felt confused as she realized that she was looking forward to seeing them. *Or am I excited about seeing Jesse?*

***

At the same time on the other side of town, an argument erupted between Blonde Mary and the owner of the Birdcage Theatre. The soiled dove was furious, staring daggers at him.

"So why not? Am I not pretty enough for you or what?"

The owner of the establishment, Hutchinson, shook his head.

"It has nothing to do with your looks, Mary! We just don't have an opening at present. The cribs downstairs are always rented out to the same three girls. Come again if one of them quits. But I have to tell you frankly that I would rather not get involved with the French syndicate that controls most of the girls and houses of ill repute on Toughnut Road. It could be dangerous for my business. Don't forget, that you are serious competition for me since you already run a brothel for them."

He crossed his arms over his chest, conveying that he had made his decision and wouldn't change his mind. Blonde Mary boiled with unconcealed anger. Her plan to lure Wild Linc into her clutches by crossing his path more often at the Birdcage had failed. And with it, the possibility of keeping a closer eye on Lorraine Bernard who frequented the theatre when she wasn't plying her trade at the Oriental Saloon was gone, too. *Well, I'll have to figure out some other way.*

The thought that Wild Linc wasn't interested in her as a future wife never crossed her mind. No, for her, it was the fault of that dark-haired witch. "If that rotten Bernard woman asked for a crib at the Birdcage, she would get it immediately," Blonde Mary hissed.

The French lady of the night wished that the cheap harlot would simply vanish from Tombstone's streets. *If not for Lorraine Bernard, Blonde Mary, could rule the red-light district, just the way she deserved to do.* Well, maybe except for the section called Hop Town. All the Chinese "lotus girls" were under China Mary's control and nobody dared mess with her, not even Blonde Mary. That Asian woman had so much influence, she even had her own Chinese police force in Tombstone.

But Blonde Mary thought she could run the rest of the red-light district. *If only I could get rid of that dang competitor.* But Lorraine had too many high-ranking contacts, and the French prostitute didn't know how to chase that soiled dove out of town.

Mary turned on her heel, cursing Hutchinson and the Birdcage Theatre in the rudest French even a sailor wouldn't have dared use. When she was gone, Hutchinson instructed one of his barkeepers to watch her whenever she set foot in his theatre. He expected further trouble from her. There was something about that woman that gave him the willies. She was madder than a rattlesnake right now and he knew she could be ruthless when she had her mind set on a certain goal.

***

Sunrise painted the sky and hills in pink and violet as Jesse rushed to Joe's cabin. He knew he was a fool but nevertheless he was excited and nervous about seeing Lorraine, even if it was for only a brief moment.

Cotton Joe greeted him with a smile and they walked over to the pretty Victorian house together.

Lorraine opened the door at the first knock and Jesse stood speechless at the sight of her. She wore a light-green dress that made her look like blossoming spring itself. Her long, wavy hair was piled in a knot showing off her swan-like neck. Jesse swallowed hard as she asked them to come into the small kitchen where a hearty breakfast awaited the surprised men.

"I'm sure I can't compete with the fish the restaurant served yesterday, but I'll feed you well before you face another hard day at the mine."

Cotton Joe laughed and winked at her. He had seen Jesse's reaction at the sight of their boss and couldn't blame him at all. The woman was a real looker and that dress accentuated her curves. He just hoped Jesse wasn't losing his heart to her. Cotton Joe had seen many a man go crazy over Lorraine, but he also knew that it was nearly impossible to conquer her heart. And Jesse awaited the arrival of his wife from Kansas.

The two prospectors enjoyed their scrambled eggs and crispy bacon that had sizzled to perfection in an iron pan. The coffee was strong, and the biscuits warm and fluffy. The kitchen was filled with mouthwatering aromas, and the atmosphere was cozy. Neither man felt like Lorraine's hired hand, as she treated each like a close friend or even family.

After finishing their meal, Lorraine handed them their wages. Jesse didn't dare count it in front of the lady. He knew it would again be a good payment as they had been able to extract even more ore out of Mother Earth than the previous week.

When they were about to leave, she let Jesse walk ahead but held her friend Joe back for a moment. "What do you think of Jesse Connor? Can we trust him?"

Cotton Joe nodded. "I would say you probably found one of the most decent guys in this whole dang town."

Lorraine thought about that for a moment. "You might as well fill him in with the truth about the hidden shaft then. He hasn't tried to spy on your section of the mine, has he?"

Cotton Joe shook his head. "No, ma'am. He stays in his shaft and works his butt off. And yes, I think he deserves to know everything about the mine. But the question is, do you want to pay him the promised full two percent share out of the gold vein as well?"

She pondered for an instant while she watched Jesse waiting patiently in the street, the orange gleam of the morning sun reflecting off his dark-brown, wavy hair.

"Well, let's make it one percent of the hidden shaft whenever he works down there. When he prospects in the other sections of the mine, he will be paid according to the original agreement. After all, we don't want to plant the seed of greed in his heart."

Cotton Joe agreed immediately. As always, Lorraine made a wise decision. Another reason why Joe admired her was her unwavering business sense.

When Cotton Joe joined him outside on the road, Jesse questioned his partner, "What was that all about?"

Cotton Joe sported his best poker face and said, "She asked if I was satisfied with your work."

"So, are you?"

Jesse had tried hard to make a good impression during his first weeks. That was plain to see. But Cotton Joe shook his head.

"I told her that you are far from perfect, and if she finds another man, she should replace you as soon as possible."

Jesse stopped right in the middle of the street, a shocked expression on his face. Then he caught the faint sound of Cotton Joe's chuckle, and soon his friend was roaring with laughter. Jesse ran after his partner, pretending to slap him. They laughed all the way to the wagon.

Lorraine watched the two men and laughed behind the window as she spotted Jesse's shocked face and Cotton Joe's chuckling. Surely Joe had pulled Jesse's leg somehow. She was happy to see how well the two men got along. Yes, she had selected the best available guy in town. From a business point of view, she was one hundred percent convinced of that.

I wonder if it is good for me to see Jesse Connor too often.
She disliked the way her heartbeat increased whenever they
met. She reminded herself that not only was he her hired
hand, but also that he was expecting his wife to arrive in
Tombstone soon. He wasn't a lonely customer hunting for
physical attention. No, Jesse Connor was a married man of
honor who stood by his word and his obligations. It would
be disastrous to mess with this proud, yet so decent fellow.

CHAPTER ELEVEN

***

Less than an hour later, the man who occupied Lorraine's thoughts was back in the shaft chiseling away, dusty but happy. He had even earned two dollars more this payday, and he expected to hear from Maggie within the next two weeks or so. Life was good for Jesse. It had been the right decision to come to Tombstone. Little did he know how fast luck could change to tragedy in the town of Tombstone.

Jesse tried his best to banish the picture of Lorraine in that lovely, spring colored dress and her swan-like neck the pinned-up hair had revealed. But no matter how hard he tried, images of her floated into his mind throughout the day.

After enjoying their lunch from the food shack, Cotton Joe announced that he had something to show Jesse. They went underground again, but this time the older fellow asked his new partner to enter Joe's section of the mine. Jesse walked behind his friend, wondering what this was all about. At the end of the small shaft Cotton Joe stopped. It was a much tighter tunnel compared to the one Jesse was working, and he wondered what could be so special about this shaft.

Joe lit another candle and regarded the young miner with a very serious expression on his face. "Swear to God and on your wife's life that you won't tell anybody what I'm going to show you."

His partner nodded but felt uneasy. When Cotton Joe turned slightly, he pointed to a spot where his chisel had marked the rock like wounds. At first Jesse didn't see any silver ore at all. It took several moments before he realized the candlelight was reflecting off a yellowish material.

"Sweet Jesus and Holy Mary, is this what I think it is?"

Cotton Joe nodded. Jesse stared at the gold vein in disbelief. *Holy cow!* Lorraine's mine was one of the smallest around Tombstone, but she had drawn the lucky ace when she had staked it. Gold and silver in a single mine. This was really rare.

Joe quickly reminded him again not to utter a single word about it to anybody, or they would probably get killed over the gold as soon as that knowledge hit the wrong characters in town. It gave Jesse goosebumps to know his friend and Lorraine would be in serious danger if this information leaked to Tombstone's saloons and brothels.

For dang sure, he would protect not only the mine but also his two new friends who had granted him an awesome start and support in Tombstone. He understood very well why they had waited for weeks before filling him in with the whole truth about their mine. It was obvious they first had to determine if he was trustworthy, and it appeared they decided this very morning that he was. Jesse had no intention of ever betraying that trust. He would be crazy to damage the source of his new and better life. Like his grandpa used to say: "Never saw off the branch you are sitting on."

No wonder Lorraine was so picky about who she hired for the mine. But not only that—now the young miner understood why she was able to pay them both an unusually generous wage and provide their daily lunch. She could afford to do so from her double strike.

But I don't understand why a wonderful woman like Lorraine would continue to offer her body as a soiled dove when she owned such a promising mine? Maybe she was indeed of loose morals? Jesse shook his head. He would probably never understand what was going on behind those huge green eyes—eyes a man could easily drown in. She must have her reasons, and who was he to question them anyway? After all, he was only a hired prospector. No more, no less.

He thanked Cotton Joe for showing him the gold shaft and promised to be even more discreet about the mine than he'd already been. He assured his partner that he would protect it with his own life if necessary. Joe patted the younger man's shoulder. He knew the secret of Lorraine's mine was safe. Not only was Jesse a decent, likeable fellow, but Joe knew something about him that so far neither Jesse nor Lorraine had realized.

He was an experienced older guy who had seen his share of life, and he had observed an important fact this morning when they had been at Lorraine's house—the spark of a fledgling love in Jesse's eyes. He might not be aware of it himself, but Cotton Joe knew that this fellow would protect the mine with everything he had because the mine represented Lorraine Bernard.

They worked hard until the early evening and, both men dwelled deeply in their own thoughts on the ride back to town. That night Jesse didn't rest well. There was still no news from Maggie, and his sleep was bothered by nightmares about thieves breaking into the mine.

When he got up from his bed, it was long before daylight. He brewed a pot of strong coffee to chase away the unpleasant pictures that lingered in his subconscious. Standing on the porch, he watched a few cardinals chasing each other. The place was so peaceful. One couldn't even imagine that there was a town so close by where people killed each other over nothing almost every day.

That particular morning, he went to work carrying an additional shotgun to the wagon. Cotton Joe frowned at him but only for an instant, then nodded. Both men knew that the possibility of a collapsing shaft wasn't the only danger they could encounter at the mine. Working together for more than two months had created a bond between them, and they understood each other without words.

The elder prospector would have never admitted it, but he had started to worry, even fear for his life, with each new gold vein he found in the smaller shaft. He was grateful for Jesse's presence, and felt mighty thankful for that additional shotgun, too.

It was good that Lorraine had insisted on hiring the newcomer. She had selected wisely. After all, it wasn't easy to find an honest man one could trust with his life in Tombstone. There were more cutthroats roaming the streets than there were fleas on a stray dog.

One never knew what would happen next in this crazy territory. For the first time in two years Cotton Joe felt the urge to drink whiskey just to calm his nerves. Of course, he wouldn't do it. Just like Jesse, he would never disappoint his boss woman's trust. It was his duty to remain sober after she had saved him from nearly drinking himself to death.

CHAPTER TWELVE

***

A month had passed since Jesse sent the letter asking Maggie to follow him out West. The weekly stagecoach from Tucson was scheduled today, and Jesse had high hopes that it would carry either his wife or her letter bearing her arrival date.

So far, the faithful husband had managed to avoid all the brothels and saloons except for visits to the fancy restaurant and a single visit to the Birdcage Theatre for a little light entertainment. Watching women singing and dancing wasn't prohibited for a married man, was it?

He had avoided all the gambling places and steadfastly saved for his future. The mining work was so backbreaking that he wasn't willing to throw his earnings away on a game of faro or poker, or even spend it in the arms of a soiled dove like most other miners did. He had been brought up with the Bible and knew that those kinds of pleasures only led to troubles.

Despite his urgent need for female tenderness, he stayed away from the women of ill repute. He didn't want to cheat on Maggie or embarrass her in any way when she came to join him. *But hell, it was about time she showed up.*

Jesse had calculated the time his letter would have taken to reach her in Kansas and the time it would take her to get ready to move out West. He knew how long the trip by train and stagecoach was to get to Tombstone. With all that in mind he knew she would either be on this week's stagecoach or at the latest, the following week. They had been separated for months since he had left his home soil, and enough was enough. After all, he was only a man. He had plenty of offers from the ladies of the night. And, like any man, he had physical needs.

His torso was hard and muscular now, his legs long and strong, his face tanned. And what the fallen angels of Toughnut Street didn't know was his stack of money grew weekly along with his muscles. Unlike others he was indeed successful as a miner.

Lorraine helped him open a bank account. It made perfect sense when she mentioned the built-in security factor of a safe and lawmen who kept an eye on the bank.

His adobe house could be robbed any time while he was gone, and he wasn't willing to risk that. Jesse had worked so hard to accumulate that money, and he needed it for his future with Maggie. *Heck, I'm even planning on raising children soon. Hope my wife agrees to that.*

***

The lonely miner called it a day a bit earlier than usual so he could meet the weekly stagecoach from Tucson late that afternoon. Jesse waited close to the post office where it would stop. He paced up and down the dusty boardwalk, as nervous as he had been when first courting Maggie.

Before going into town Jesse washed himself at the creek near the mine, wanting to look as decent as possible after the dirty work underground. Maggie always paid attention to looks. Soon Maggie would be climbing out of the coach, or he would receive a nice, loving letter from her that still carried a trace of her perfume. Jesse really missed his wife, and it showed in his nervous, inpatient behavior. He wasn't aware that Lorraine watched him from the window of her little house across the street. The sad smile on her face faded as she slowly lowered the lace curtain again.

"Looks like he is expecting news from her, or maybe even her arrival," she mumbled into the empty room.

How thrilled, how happy he looked. *I envy the woman,* Lorraine thought bitterly. But she knew she had no right to interfere in this relationship. It seemed to be a happy marriage. She wondered what the woman was like who had captured the heart of such a fine man. Was she beautiful? She must be. Lorraine knew that he had resisted every soiled dove in town. *Takes a hell of a woman for a man to be so faithfully to her.*

She turned away from the window and decided to go to the Oriental Saloon that evening. It was time to tend to her own business. Jesse Connor was one of the few men who was out of Lorraine's reach. Even worse, he was the only man whom she regretted was unattainable.

"For the first time in all these years I wish I lived a different life, one with a husband like Jesse," she whispered sadly into the silent living room. Suddenly her beautiful furniture didn't mean much to her anymore.

Upon hearing the loud rattling noises from the red stagecoach, she returned to the window. Although her mind told her to turn away from the scene, she couldn't bring herself to walk away from the window. She gazed through the curtain and watched Jesse jumping from one foot to the other next to the stagecoach.

He tore open the coach's door before the horses came to a complete stop. Five dusty, exhausted passengers climbed stiffly out of the coach, two women and three men. Jesse's handsome features showed bleak disappointment when he realized none of the ladies were his wife Maggie.

As the porter unloaded the luggage, he tossed a big sack of mail to the ground. It landed right in front Jesse's boots, raising a cloud of dust. The impatient lad would have to wait at the post office until the fellow there had sorted through it all.

Jesse had always been a well-balanced and patient person, but his patience teetered standing next to the sweating horses. He threw the sack of mail over his shoulder and carried it into the post office himself. He bribed the employee there with an extra dollar to increase his speed going through it while he paced back and forth like a hungry lion. His boot heels reverberated loudly on the wood floor of the cramped room, and the postal officer looked up from his work countless times, scowling.

Finally, the post employee waved a thick envelope at him. "Mister Connor, Jesse Connor?"

"Yes, sir, that's me."

"Well, looks like I've got your expected letter here. This is a mighty thick envelope if you'll allow me to say so."

Jesse took it, smiling broadly now. He thanked the man and left the building. As he walked out into the late afternoon sun clutching the urgently expected letter, he intended to go home to read it. But curiosity got the better of him and he decided to open Maggie's letter right away.

He had waited for news from his wife much too long to waste more time riding home first. He decided to walk over to Cotton Joe's place and sit on the porch. As soon as he arrived, he tore open the sealed envelope.

Cotton Joe, who saw his approach through the open front door, came outside and handed him a glass of cold lemonade. Then he nodded and turned around, giving Jesse privacy to read the long-awaited love letter.

When he opened it, he was surprised but happy to find quite a few pages to read. The first page bore Maggie's neat, scrolled handwriting. He had always admired it.

"My dearest Jesse, I trust this letter finds you in good health. I have received the good news about your mining job and the successful settling down in the town of Tombstone, and I am, of course, happy for you."

Happy for me? He shook his head. She should be happy for both of us. But he continued to read. He wasn't aware that Cotton Joe watched him through the kitchen window and worried about the frown showing on Jesse's handsome features. The longer he read, the more it seemed as if dark clouds covered his friend's face.

"As you know, my dear husband, I never really agreed to move out West into the hostile Sonoran Desert with you, but as I failed to change your mind, I was at least willing to give it a try.

"I saw it as my duty as a wedded wife to follow my husband wherever he would go. However, during the months of separation and living with my parents I have come to the conclusion that the kind of life you have chosen would never be the right one for me.

"I just cannot imagine living there and leaving my family behind. With a heavy heart, and believe me, this decision was not an easy one for me to make, I have decided to stay in Kansas with my family. Forgive me, but I cannot follow you to the Arizonan territory.

"Enclosed in this letter you will find papers from the lawyers Campbell and Sons which will legally dissolve this marriage. Please sign them and send them back to me as fast as possible."

What in the world? Jesse sat there, rubbing his eyes. He couldn't believe what he was reading. It must be some dust from the mine in his eyes obscuring his vision.

By now Cotton Joe had stepped out onto the porch but Jesse was unaware. He was still reading, starting over again from the last section of the letter, hoping and praying that his eyes played a nasty trick on him.

"Enclosed in this letter you will find papers from the lawyers Campbell and Sons which will legally dissolve this marriage. Please sign them and send them back to me as fast as possible.

"I know you may be sad or even angry with me, but please see it as a favor because I'm setting you free to live the life of an adventurer that you always wished for. I am not made for a life in a rough Western pioneer town away from my own folks and civilization. My family has agreed to take care of me for the time being so you don't have to worry about my well-being anymore. Please don't try to come see me or to talk me out of this. I have made up my mind and won't change my decision.

"In my opinion, this marriage has been a mistake right from the beginning. We just don't really match. God knows I wish you all the best in your life, but I won't be part of it any longer. Your former wife, Maggie."

The hand holding the letter dropped slowly into his lap, his eyes looked out at Allen Street but he didn't see a dang thing. Jesse was blinded by his own tears. Those strong hands that had chiseled so much money out of the rocks for a better life with his beloved wife hadn't been strong enough prevent her from leaving him. All the work, the hardship, the dreaming, and trying to do his best—it was all in vain. He looked down at the other papers. They were official documents from a lawyer's office by the name of Campbell and Sons.

Cotton Joe didn't know what was written in the letter but he saw the official papers and knew that this was far from the kind of message Jesse had anticipated for so many weeks. Joe gently touched his young friend on the shoulder. Jesse got up slowly, like an old man and turned around to hand Cotton Joe his empty glass. Jesse couldn't recall when he had drunk the lemonade. He felt numb and empty. The older man tried to say something but Jesse held up his hand.

"Not now, Joe, not now."

He turned around and staggered off across Allen Street, the letter forgotten in his hand, his face a stony mask with sad, watery eyes. The pain hadn't settled in with full force but it would.

CHAPTER THIRTEEN

***

Cotton Joe was concerned. He saw his friend walking toward the cheaper saloons and brothels on Toughnut Street and didn't like it at all. He would follow the greenhorn, but first he went back into the house and hid a small derringer pistol under his jacket.

The caring friend walked along Toughnut Street and around the corner toward Allen Street, but Jesse was nowhere to be seen. A deep frown on Cotton Joe's face showed how worried he was. It was getting dark and only God knew what the guy was up to after receiving what was obviously bad news. *All I can do now is to get help from our best friend in town to look for the lad. I need to find Lorraine.*

The Calico Queen had just finished singing a love song and mingled with the guests at the poker table. Wild Linc was playing cards today, and he was in a bad mood from losing a considerable amount of money. He was unfriendly and rude to everybody in the saloon, even to Lorraine.

She tried her best to cheer him up and tenderly rubbed

his neck while standing behind him, watching the game. She wasn't in the mood for male company tonight but forced herself to remain at the Oriental trying to forget how happy and excited Jesse had been waiting for the stagecoach.

The sight left her upset. *I don't know what bothers me more—him being so thrilled about news from his wife, or me reacting to it with pure jealousy,* she wondered while watching the game of poker.

This was getting out of control, and she had to make sure she didn't forget her philosophy. Lorraine had her own rules and would adhere to them regardless of who or what crossed her path. In a soiled dove's life, it was all about self-protection.

"You made yourself pretty rare lately, Bernard!" Wild Linc Duncan complained. But he was no match for the beautiful lady's clever charms.

"Why now, did you miss me, handsome?"

He was flattered by her tender way of addressing him. He wrapped one of his strong arms around her hips while the other held a hand of promising-looking cards. He planned to take her into one of the private cribs close to the poker table when Cotton Joe came rushing into the saloon.

Lorraine sensed that something was wrong. She knew her mining partner avoided all saloons and brothels so as not to be tempted into drinking. He must have a urgent reason to show up at the Oriental, and she didn't like his worried expression. Lorraine left Wild Linc sitting where he was and rushed over to talk to Joe.

Duncan cursed rudely after her, obviously hopping mad at being abandoned for some other guy. He watched Cotton Joe whisper something into his favorite soiled dove's ear and was about to jump up and assure the fellow that he, Wild Linc, was first in line tonight.

But then Linc saw the deep concern on her gorgeous face as she whirled around, grasping her shawl and heading for the door right away. Without even looking back she followed that older chap out on the street. Wild Linc shook with barely hidden anger while the other guys at the poker table laughed.

"Looks like you're not her favorite man tonight, Linc!"

Duncan jumped up, sending his chair flying backwards. He held his knife in his hand, ready to slash out at the man who made jokes on his account. But the others held him back, and the owner of the saloon ordered them to throw Duncan out of the Oriental for the night.

"Go home, sober up, and don't you dare to come back as long as you plan to attack my guests, Wild Linc!"

Everybody in town knew how hot tempered and danger-ous the guy was when things didn't go the way he wanted, so the people near the poker table avoided stepping in his way. Wild Linc turned around, shaking his fist in the di-rection of the saloon owner.

Lincoln Duncan's anger wasn't about being thrown out of the premises. He was more upset about Lorraine letting him down again. She made him look like a fool tonight and that was unacceptable. It was about time he taught her a lesson she wouldn't forget. A dangerous spark appeared in his steely blue eyes.

***

Lorraine's voice shook as she and Joe crossed Allen Street. "What happened? Where is he?"

"I have no clue, Lorraine. He got this letter and it looked like something official, then he stood and walked away. I wanted to hold him back but, he wouldn't talk to me at all."

"Don't feel guilty, Joe. I know you tried your best. Now

let's go find him."

They split up and walked along the crowded streets of Tombstone. Fights around this time of night got more violent and often ended deadly over something as simple as a lousy hand of cards or a cheap bottle of whiskey, so they both were on highest alert.

The fallen angel was very concerned about the events. Something troublesome must be written in that letter, and she wondered if one of Jesse's relations had passed away. It was a shame that she knew so little about the man who worked for her.

As Lorraine walked by the French portion of the devil's section of town, she overheard two ladies of the line talking about Blonde Mary.

"She sure was lucky to lay her hands on this handsome guy. Have seen him around town but he never came to be with any of us."

The other girl laughed.

"Well, sooner or later, they all get weak. They got him drunk as well, so I guess he won't be much of a lover tonight. But Lord, his body is to die for."

Lorraine had the strong feeling the women of easy virtue were speaking about Jesse. Although she knew she risked being beaten by the French prostitutes, she entered the house of easy virtue run by Blonde Mary.

She immediately saw Jesse leaning against the bar. It wasn't his drunken state that shocked her, but the empty, sad expression on his face. She had never seen him like this.

"What do you think you're doing here?" The icy, cold voice of Blonde Mary hissed at her from behind the bar.

"I'll take my friend home now," Lorraine calmly explained.

"I reckon you won't! Either you remove your filthy

ass out from my place, or I'll teach you a lesson about plucking fruits from another person's garden. You think you can steal all my men, Bernard? Well, let me tell you straight to your face, if you don't keep your dirty hands off my Johns, I'll kill you."

The room went dead silent. Jesse didn't speak a single word. The door opened, and in walked Cotton Joe, his derringer in his hand with the hammer cocked back.

"I am here to pick up my partner. He has to sober up for work tomorrow, and you, Blonde Mary, better not get in our way. You had your share of fun. It's time to call it a day."

With a determined expression he grasped Jesse by the belt, pulling him toward the front door while still aiming his derringer at Blonde Mary. The French prostitute's face was pale, and she shook with fury. Cotton Joe pointed his chin toward the door and called Lorraine over.

"Let's leave. Time for all of us to go home and get some shut eye."

Lorraine was relieved that her friend had showed up armed just in time to save Jesse and her. The scene could have gone wrong, but she had taken the risk for Jesse without thinking twice about it. *By God, I really care for him,* she realized with a sad smile.

Cotton Joe suggested bringing their drunken friend to his cabin where he would help him get back on his feet. Lorraine agreed and together they undressed Jesse.

After they had tossed a few buckets of cold water over him, they tried to sober him up further with pots of strong, black coffee. Jesse was pale and sat shivering on Joe's bunkbed as he sipped the steaming beverage.

As Lorraine folded his clothes, a letter fell out of his shirt pocket. She picked it up, not intending to read it. Spying on others wasn't her style, but something catastrophic must have shocked her hired hand, and she wanted to know what it was.

With shaking hands, she unfolded the papers and started to read. As she finished the letter, she was numb with shock. Now she understood how devastated he must feel. The guy who had tried so hard to provide his wife with a good life, and worked tremendously hard for it had been betrayed in the cruelest way. *His better half who he tried to make happy had let him down like a coward, not even willing to speak to him face-to-face, not even willing to work things out.* Lorraine shook her head in disbelief.

When a sound behind her pulled her out of her gloomy thoughts, she slowly turned around to stare right into Jesse's face. He looked at the letter in her trembling hands. Lorraine held it up in her hand.

"I'm sorry. It fell out of your shirt. I didn't mean to snoop through your private things." But he didn't answer. A broken heart peered through the cold eyes in the handsome features. It saddened Lorraine that she couldn't find the Jesse Connor she had known.

Cotton Joe had seen his own share of heartache. He was angry with that spoiled filly who had broken the heart of one of the most decent and honest men he had ever met. His friendship with Jesse was sincere, and he swore to himself to do everything possible to return a smile to the guy's face. Dang, he deserved a happier life.

It was Cotton Joe's turn to bring back happier days to his friend just as Lorraine had done for Joe years ago. No, he wasn't willing to watch Jesse feeling down or even worse, destroy himself.

Lorraine Bernard was an outstanding woman. But unlike him, she didn't know about all the dark moments that could turn a man into a drinker or opium abuser. Joe knew about those lonely hours too well, when the devil lures a man into selling his soul. He would move heaven and earth to prevent this fine young man from walking down the same devastating path that he had travelled two years back.

Joe and Lorraine agreed to take Jesse under their protective wings. At this point, a former drinker and the highest priced prostitute of Tombstone were the only family Jesse Connor had left.

CHAPTER FOURTEEN

* * *

The next morning brought head splitting cruelty. Jesse sat up and felt terrible. His head throbbed, he was nauseated, and it took him a few moments to realize he wasn't in his own cabin.

Then he remembered the letter, and his heart sank. Jesse still couldn't believe it. His wife had left him. What in the world had he done wrong to cause her to make such a devastating decision without even speaking to him? *Had she planned this all along after he left Kansas? Had she considered following him out West at all?*

What a fool he was believing in a woman who had never really cared for him. "I should have known better," he mumbled. His friend Cotton Joe came into the room with a smile and a pot of coffee.

"Come on over to the table, son. Here's some coffee and scrambled eggs for you. We can start work a bit later today."

Jesse made a snorting sound. "Work? What for? It's all in vain anyway."

Cotton Joe shook his head. "I wouldn't see it so negatively. You should be proud of yourself, young man! Yes, proud about everything you've achieved since coming to this God-forsaken town. Nobody can take that away from you. And eventually you'll find a woman who's willing to live her life with you and to support your dreams and is really worthy of your love. As I understand things, your so-called wife never really had your back anyway."

Jesse should have been angry with Joe for speaking so rudely about Maggie, but he knew the older man told the truth. She had never really cherished him as a husband, and he had always been the one who tried to impress and please her. Shouldn't that be a two-way street?

"How did you find me last night? I don't even remember where I was."

"It wasn't me. Lorraine found you. It was fortunate she did, I must say. She risked her neck to bail you out of that French prostitute's fangs. But I backed her up with my gun. Quite risky to mess around with the French red-light fellers."

"Lorraine saw me like this? Oh, for land's sake!"

Cotton Joe shook his head. "Don't worry. She knows that such things happen. The main thing is that we get you back on your feet. Consider coming back to work at the mine at least. Look at becoming as rich and successful as possible as some sort of sweet revenge so that your wife, pardon me, former wife bites her own spoiled 'derriere' for leaving such a wonderful gentleman."

Jesse looked at his friend, at first not convinced, but the longer he thought about it, the more he realized that Cotton Joe was right. Slowly, but surely, a new ambition replaced his original goal of working for his future with Maggie.

This time it wasn't love that fueled his energy. Instead, hate and the wish for revenge consumed him. Then a second thought crossed his mind. Lorraine had risked a lot to make sure he was safe last night. He truly appreciated that lady. She had done more for him than any other person he had encountered in life. He owed her a great deal.

Jesse was a strong man but he knew the wound that Maggie's betrayal had inflicted wouldn't heal easily. He would never be the same after this disappointment. All his hopes, or rather illusions, were shattered yesterday.

***

Lorraine woke up early after a restless night. She worried about Jesse, and the threats from Blonde Mary had left her nervous. It went way beyond the usual "jealousy among prostitutes" behavior. Something in that crazy woman's eyes bothered her. *Jesus, she had threatened to kill me.* She had no clue why Blonde Mary hated her so much, but Lorraine knew she had to watch her back from now on. *I'm sure I embarrassed Blonde Mary in her own territory. No fallen angel has a forgiving mentality when it comes to that.*

It wasn't the first time Lorraine had encountered this kind of threat and knew that women of easy morals often were unpredictable in their actions. She decided to talk to some of the girls around Toughnut Street. Maybe it was possible to find out what had triggered Blonde Mary's extreme revulsion toward her.

As she left her house, Lorraine glanced over to Cotton Joe's and saw that he and Jesse were about to leave for the mine. She resisted the urge to walk over and check on her hired miners. Maybe it was better to give Jesse some time alone to come to terms with the divorce. By now he must know that she had been the one who saved him from being robbed at the French bordello. The whole situation was hard enough for him, and she didn't want to add to his embarrassment.

The wagon rumbled along the street and out of town. It was good for the poor lad to go back to work. Lorraine breathed a sigh of relief knowing that her older partner would keep an eye on Jesse today.

When she could no longer see the wagon, she turned and headed toward the red-light district on Sixth Street. She wanted to ask some questions of the women of easy virtue. "I also have to make up with Lincoln Duncan. Last night I completely forgot about him after leaving the Oriental Saloon in such a hurry," she mumbled, hurrying down the street.

He wasn't an important customer, and she wouldn't miss him if he dropped her despite his lovemaking abilities. But he could be a dangerous man when rejected. Lorraine had to play it diplomatically to give him the feeling that he should give up on her, not the other way around.

Maybe she could get him interested in another girl. *I have to find the fresh soiled doves who arrived in town a few weeks back. It won't be easy but I'll give it a try. It's about time to get rid of Wild Linc for good.* Little did she know that Lincoln Duncan felt possessiveness toward her, and wasn't at all willing to give up on Lorraine.

As she walked through Sixth Street some of the women stared at her. They envied Lorraine for her influence in the red-light district. Those selling their bodies in the cheap cribs had to serve every dirty, stinking customers with terrible breath. Some of the soiled doves were sick despite the monthly disease control ordered by the town. Most of them didn't get enough food, and their bodies showed the abuse of laudanum or symptoms of consumption. Their coughs followed Lorraine like a cruel echo of death.

Lorraine selected three girls that looked much too skinny and took them to the food shack to buy warm meals for them. Most likely it was the first decent food they'd had in days. At first the women were distrusting and cautious, but their hunger conquered their fears.

While they wolfed down the food, Lorraine asked a few careful questions about Blonde Mary's disturbing behavior. In the beginning it was difficult to break the ice, but one of the girls opened up. It was hard to understand her speech, interrupted by intense coughing spells and wheezing. Lorraine pitied the girl, who must have been in her early twenties.

"Well, lady, you stole Blonde Mary's lover. That is, at least she claims so. I have my doubts about her version of the story because I know Wild Linc has been seeing you much longer than her, or any other shady lady. And quite often for that matter. But she has this silly idea about marrying him."

Lorraine couldn't believe what she heard. Again, Wild Linc was the heart of the problem. It was time to cut their connection. The man meant nothing but trouble.

The other women dared to share their parts of the story, now that their companion had spilled the beans.

"She actually tells everybody that she'll kill you if you don't keep your hands off her man. And to make it worse, Wild Linc tells everybody in town that you're his legal woman. We are quite certain Blonde Mary means every word. You better be careful!"

Lorraine's hands closed into strong fists. "Lies, nothing but lies," she muttered under her breath. "Well, I wish they would settle for each other and leave me alone. They're both crazier than loons and deserve each other. I just want to be at peace and done with both of them. I never considered myself Linc's woman. As a matter of fact, I am *nobody's* woman."

The other three women laughed. They thanked her for the meal and emphasized that they had to get back to work. "We are losing too many coins if we don't go back to the cribs now." Since Lorraine was a generous and caring person, she gave them all a dollar to cover their lost time. The fallen angels were surprised, and one almost cried, but when they walked away, they appeared happy about the unexpected gift. They knew they would never be in a position to earn as much as Lorraine did.

The popular shady lady couldn't believe it. *That silly French whore dares to threaten me. And Wild Linc is nothing but a rotten piece of dirt who has neither his desires nor his filthy, lying mouth under control.*

It was about time she showed them both that she wasn't a person to be pushed around as if she were some sort of toy. She was Lorraine Bernard and ruled her own life. Those who got on her wrong side were making a big mistake. She had to come up with a plan to get Wild Linc away from her for good. She went over to Judge Taylor's house, hoping he could identify a legal strategy to ban that possessive jerk from her life.

***

Meanwhile, Cotton Joe and Jesse worked hard at the mine. The despondent young man lacked motivation at first, but soon the wish for revenge accelerated his work speed. By the time they were finished that evening, he had chiseled out more rock in one day than ever before. However, for the first time, he wasn't proud of his efforts. His original incentive, a better life with Maggie, had been wrenched away. He couldn't imagine what the future held for him.

Future? What future do I have now?

Exhausted, he went straight home after work. His friend understood that Jesse wanted to be alone. Cotton Joe didn't force unwanted conversation on him. Instead Joe went to Lorraine's and reported on how their young friend was doing.

The lady of the night had a story to tell her partner, too. She filled him in on the latest news from the red-light district, and Joe expressed his concern for her well-being.

"Looks like I'll have to babysit both of you for different reasons now," he growled through his red beard.

She laughed at him. "Don't worry, my dear friend, I can protect myself pretty well. I'm a big girl. But it's good that you know the truth just in case I need you for back up again. I'll try to solve the problem with Linc and Blonde Mary as quickly as I can. Judge Taylor said he'd help as well."

CHAPTER FIFTEEN

***

Wild Linc sat at a remote table in the corner of one of the smaller saloons on the south side of Allen Street. He'd been drinking since early afternoon, and people avoided crossing his path. It was obvious he was in a dangerous mood. No one wanted to poke the hornet's nest, so everyone stayed clear.

Linc blamed the handsome stranger for Lorraine's recent cool behavior. He had to make sure that guy left town. But he couldn't just shoot him, or Lorraine might never speak to him again. No, he'd have to lure the fellow into a trap.

Somehow, Wild Linc had to convince the woman that the stranger wasn't worth her trust. But so far, he hadn't come up with a promising solution to the problem. And the longer it took, the more influence that young fellow had on Linc's favorite soiled dove and her affection toward him.

Just like Blonde Mary, Wild Linc was always quick to blame others whenever he failed. The ruthless man would never have considered the possibility that a woman wasn't interested in a deeper relationship with him. He was so self-centered that believed he was irresistible to the female world of Tombstone, maybe even the entirety of Cochise County. Admittedly, he was a handsome man, and the ladies of the night swarmed to him like bees around the honey pot. But Wild Linc had seen the fear in their faces during his spells of contemptuous and aggressive behavior.

For the first time in Linc Duncan's life a woman had rejected his charms and perhaps lost interest in him. He had never experienced treatment such as that before, and it felt like a wasp's sting. His ego suffered tremendously and set free the mean and unpredictable beast within.

When he rose to leave the saloon, staggering on unsteady legs, he still lacked a plan about how to sabotage Jesse Connor. *I am a smart man and will come up with* some way *soon enough.* As he stepped through the saloon's door, his eyes squinted against the glaring sun, and he glanced down Allen Street to the small home where Cotton Joe lived. Slowly a cruel smile stretched Wild Linc's lips. Yes, that was a possibility. It had been there all the time, right in front of his eyes.

He'd make sure that Lorraine would end up hating Jesse Connor, and then she'd be his for good, at least as long as he was interested in her. One never knew how long that would be when it came to women.

In a much better mood, the handsome gambler felt an urge to celebrate, so he went over to the French quarter of the red-light district. Oh, yes, he'd make the best out of this wonderful evening.

He didn't want to cavort with Blonde Mary—that woman was as dangerous as a rattlesnake—but maybe with a couple of the younger ones. It didn't take long for him to find two willing Mademoiselles. He paid their price, and all three disappeared into one of the lush bordellos.

Meanwhile, Lorraine enjoyed a delicious dinner at Judge

Taylor's house. She wasn't hungry but tried her best to be social and keep the judge happy. Carefully, she led the conversation toward Wild Linc and the way he threatened her. "His lies are creating real trouble for me around the red-light district."

The judge, being a perfect gentleman, immediately promised to take action against the villain. "Dear Lorraine, you must understand that I need to find a legitimate reason to arrest him. I can't have him locked up in the pokey for nothing. We need proof that he is guilty of some crime."

The elegant woman thought about that. She knew Judge Taylor was an honest, decent man of the law, and he would never sign a warrant against someone if a true crime hadn't been committed. She had to think of something.

She didn't like setting a trap for Wild Linc and knew it would be risky if Linc ever discovered her plotting. Nobody in town doubted that Linc Duncan was capable of sending someone to the bone orchard if he was mad enough. But getting him arrested seemed to be the only way out of the unpleasant situation.

Difficult tasks lay ahead, and she decided to skip entertaining clients until she came up with a promising plan. Too much was at stake.

***

Blonde Mary was boiling with anger when she heard of Wild Linc's threesome adventure. The only thing that calmed her was the knowledge that he hadn't spent the time in that Bernard woman's bed.

A treacherous smile curved her lips upward, and turned her face into a distorted mask. Yes, Lorraine Bernard was definitely losing ground. That thought lifted Blonde Mary's mood immensely for the moment, but just like Wild Linc, she had an unpredictable temper.

The next morning Jesse arrived at Cotton Joe's cabin on time for work. His mining partner tried to engage him in a conversation but Jesse remained silent with a stern expression on his face. Cotton Joe wasn't upset about it. He knew there were times when a man had to withdraw to his mental cave.

The two friends worked hard the entire day, and Cotton Joe allowed Jesse to prospect in the gold shaft for the first time since Lorraine had hired him. Joe intended to cheer the guy up, but even gold mining didn't help to lift his mood.

Jesse signed the divorce papers and sent them back. He was done with the woman who had broken his heart so cruelly. However, it would take much longer for him to process his feelings about the demise of his marriage and overcome the bitter pain she had caused him.

In the evening the men sat together on Joe's porch and enjoyed a cold glass of lemonade. Jesse turned to face his partner.

"Joe, I want to apologize. I know I've been a grouchy companion of late, but I can assure you it will get better eventually."

Joe patted his younger friend on the shoulder. "You take all the time you need, Jesse. It won't change my opinion of you. You have a painful heartache to over-come. I know that."

Jesse looked at him, and asked, "Have you ever been married?"

Cotton Joe laughed out loud. "Why, yes of course, why do you think I started drinking?" Cotton Joe an-swered dryly.

Jesse laughed, but it was a bitter sound.

"My wife died of smallpox. There wasn't anything I

could do to save her. I buried her next to our four-year-old daughter."

Cotton Joe stared into the open space, haunted by old memories.

"Jesus, I am sorry, Joe. I shouldn't have asked." Jesse was embarrassed.

But Joe shook his head. "I was alone when it happened, and I went down, all the way to hell. But you, my dear friend, you are not alone. You have friends, Lorraine, and me. We won't let you down. I like you a lot; heck, I even see you as a younger brother now."

Jesse was deeply touched and promised Cotton Joe that he would try to get himself together as quickly as possible. Joe pointed toward the saloons and red-light district. "You're already doing a good job if you avoid those buildings over there, son."

Jesse nodded. "You're right. I won't find healing there. Well, I'd better call it a day. Time to go home and hit the sack. See you tomorrow, Joe."

Cotton Joe waved goodbye as Jesse hoisted his tired body into the saddle of his patiently waiting mare.

"He didn't even mention the gold he dug out of the mine today. The poor guy is really down," mumbled Cotton Joe to himself. He could only hope that his partner would feel better soon. Jesse had become a good friend, and Cotton Joe knew firsthand how much rockier the road back to a decent life was compared to going downhill.

Once again, Joe cursed the ruthless woman for sending her cruel letter and hoped she would run into the kind of saphead she really deserved as a husband. She was obviously selfish and spoiled rotten and didn't deserve a decent fellow like Jesse to give her a good life.

**

The next few days went by uneventfully. Lorraine had hardly appeared at the Oriental Saloon or the Birdcage Theatre and avoided Wild Linc as much as possible.

Blonde Mary was busy recruiting some new French girls who had arrived a few days back with the "cat wagon," as they called the stage that brought in new soiled doves.

Cotton Joe and Jesse took care of their own business working the mine. Neither Lorraine nor her two friends were aware of the trouble that brewed on the horizon.

CHAPTER SIXTEEN

***

Monsoon season had arrived in Cochise County. Jesse was surprised how powerfully destructive the rain and thunderstorms could be in this area. After all, Cochise County was normally dry as a bone.

Cotton Joe's wagon was caught in one of the spring floods blocking a wash on their way back into town. It took a great deal of coaxing to convince the horses to wade through the water where it was shallow enough to cross with the wagon.

Not without a certain pride, Jesse saw that the repaired roof of his cozy house withstood all the rain storms that hit the area. But then he remembered that he had worked so hard on the building for his wife Maggie, and the good mood vanished like the cool dawn air after sunrise.

There was no point in rubbing salt into an open wound by recalling their few happy moments together. It was over. He had to move on, and he constantly reminded himself of that fact.

His savings steadily grew, and he had great new friends. But Jesse was a very lonely man who had lost his vision of a better tomorrow. The prospector didn't know which was worse—being alone as a man or having nothing to look forward to. Both hurt equally.

Countless nights he lay awake despite the fatigue in his body. Again and again he wondered if he could have done something to avoid the separation, wondered if they would still be happily married if only he had stayed back in Kansas.

But deep in his heart Jesse knew it hadn't been a happy marriage from the start. It was time to march forward and let go of the past. Maybe one day he would find another love. Maybe. *It would take a hell of a woman to heal this broken heart of mine. She'd have to be a daredevil or … maybe a lady like Lorraine Bernard?*

Jesse hadn't seen Lorraine much lately, and Cotton Joe told him that she faced some trouble with a clinging customer who behaved like a blood-sucking tick.

Jesse worried about that news but Cotton Joe assured him that he kept an eye on their "boss" and her home every day once they returned from the mine. That comforted Jesse to a certain degree, but he still worried.

The following day was a rainy, gloomy one, and the two miners could hardly make out the dirt road ahead of them as they traveled back to town. The wheels of their wagon cut deeply into the mud. Jesse helped push through washes and lead the horses when the trail was slippery.

Just as they came around a bend, three men on horseback stopped them. The exhausted miners wondered if the riders needed any help. None of them spoke, and Jesse grew nervous. He hadn't seen any of the men before, but Cotton Joe seemed to know at least one of them.

"Linc, what can we do for you guys?" he asked coolly. *Doesn't look as if Joe likes that tall feller a lot,* Jesse mused.

Wild Linc had a sinister look. "Well, Cotton Joe, you could help me get rid of my competitor here," and pointed at Jesse, an unfriendly expression on his face. Joe frowned, but Jesse had no clue what this was about.

"Linc, we don't want any trouble. We're tired, it's been a long day, and we'd really appreciate it if you wouldn't block the trail any longer. All we want is to drive this wagon back home before we get stuck in the mud again."

Cotton Joe had spoken in a calm, even manner. But then, without any warning, Linc Duncan pulled his six-shooter and fired. A blazing flame appeared in the barrel of the gun, followed by the loud boom of a gunshot spooking the horses.

Jesse jumped from his seat as Cotton Joe fell backwards and let go of the reins with a grunting sound.

"Joe! Nooooo!" Jesse shouted, trying to catch his friend as he fell from the bench. Joe's face wore a mask of disbelief and shock. Before Jesse could react to what had just happened, the butt of a shotgun smacked against his temple, and the world turned black as he fell off the wagon.

***

Unsure about how much time had passed, the next thing Jesse was aware of was the sound of dripping water in a steady, nerve-wracking rhythm. When he opened his eyes, it caused a stabbing pain in his head. Dizzy and sick, Jesse realized that it was dark around him, and he lay on hard-packed dirt. The air smelled of damp soil. He had no clue where he was and tried hard to recall what had happened, but his memory failed. A splitting headache left him nauseated.

He heard the voices of two men talking in the distance.

"Why didn't we just shoot him, Linc?"

"Well, you idiot, she would be sorry and sad about it then. No, I want her to hate him, not mourn over him. I want her to suspect he was the one who shot her dear friend Cotton Joe. So we have to hide him until she finds out what happened. If things go right, he'll stand trial, and I can wash my hands of his death. The lawdog will help me get rid of him through legal channels."

Wild Linc made a cruel sound, a lunatic kind of laugh.

"You are obsessed with this woman. It'll break your neck one day, I swear. Well, Linc, I've paid my dues. Now give me and my brother our money, then we're out of here. Heading toward Mexico. It wouldn't be good to be seen around you until this whole case blows over."

"You're right; here you go. Your silver as promised. Make sure you save some of the pretty señoritas for me down there."

"You betcha," the other fellow promised.

"Sooner or later, you'll lose interest in that Bernard woman anyway."

Jesse tried to follow the conversation but suddenly the place went dead silent. The outlaws must have departed. He was fully awake now, but his head hurt, and he couldn't think straight.

It looked like he was being held prisoner in an old shed or maybe a stable. he was so dizzy that he had to close his eyes to stop the room from spinning. Suddenly he heard the sound of boots tramping on the dirt floor, then felt a brutal kick to his gut.

"You rotten piece of shit, thought you could get in my way and steal Lorraine, didn't you?"

Jesse didn't answer.

"Well, let me tell you, when she finds out that you're gone and her mining partner was shot, she'll put two and two together and that'll be the end of your friendship with *my* woman. She'll hate you and might even see to it herself that you meet the hangman. You'll probably be dead when she gets through with you. What an irony of destiny. The one who helped you get started in this town will be the very person to throw you into hell where you belong. And then the path will be clear for me to catch that little bird once and for all. You should've never gotten in Linc Duncan's way, you stupid fool. It would have been better if you had never set foot in Tombstone."

Jesse wasn't sure if he understood what the guy was talking about, but slowly a cruel image of Cotton Joe falling off the wagon with a bullet in his torso formed in his head. The memory increased the sickening throbbing in his temple.

For sakes alive, now I remember. They stopped us on the way back from the mine, then without a warning there was a shot. What happened to Cotton Joe? Was he dead? He must be.

An immense sadness filled Jesse's heart. Joe had been his best friend in town. Even more so, the best friend he'd ever had in his entire life.

"I'll get even for this. I swear, if it's the last thing I do in this world."

Jesse's vision blurred and his heart raced. The fury in his chest spread like a burning fire on the open range. Wild Linc laughed like a mad man.

"Well guess what, dude? It looks like right now I'm holding the better hand of cards. You won't escape, and I plan to bring you into town myself as the murderer of Cotton Joe. But first, I'll make sure you appear to be 'in hiding' for a few days after the terrible crime you committed."

CHAPTER SEVENTEEN

***

Lorraine paced nervously in the parlor of her house. She had expected Cotton Joe and Jesse hours ago to give them their weekly payment. They hadn't shown up, and it was growing dark. The fallen angel had a well-trained intuition despite her young age, and she sensed that something was terribly wrong. As she pondered whether she should ask someone to ride out to the mine or, if she should ride there herself, turmoil broke out down Allen Street.

At first Lorraine thought it was the usual bar fight erupting into the street in front of the saloons, but then she saw Cotton Joe's empty wagon rumbling along the street. The horses ran straight to the little log cabin, the home they knew so well. But strangely, nobody was in the wagon's seat.

Lorraine frantically pulled up her skirts, running across the street to Joe's cabin. She worked at calming the nervous horses, but they snorted with wide eyes and flared nostrils. They must have run along the trail for quite a distance as both animals were lathered with sweat.

Where the heck are Cotton Joe and Jesse Connor? Only

then Lorraine saw the curled-up figure of her dear friend Joe lying in the back of the wagon. He was terribly pale and lay on the wood planks in a dark puddle of his own blood.

She screamed for help and immediately a few men lent her a hand with the exhausted, nervous horses. Others turned the injured man onto his back.

Lorraine's voice was barely above a whisper. "Oh, my God, is he dead?"

What in the world had happened, and where was Jesse? The doctor came running, his black leather bag bouncing against his leg. He saw the blood soaking Cotton Joe's shirt, and it didn't take him long to find the cause.

"He's been shot. Too late to help him."

The doctor was about to turn away, but Lorraine heard a faint moan and called after the sawbones. "Doctor Good-fellow, come back, please! I think he's still alive. You have to remove the bullet."

Doc Goodfellow checked for a pulse and nodded. "Bring him over to my house but be careful—his pulse is very weak. Don't twist his upper torso. We don't want to move that bullet. It looks like it might be stuck mighty close to his lung."

Lorraine held Cotton Joe's clammy hand. *Where in God's name, is Jesse? Had he been shot as well? Had they been ambushed at the mine?* Too many questions bombarded her mind while she worried for the life of her closest friend.

Cotton Joe lay on the table at Doctor Goodfellow's place. He moaned again as the doctor probed the gunshot wound. The beautiful fallen angel was at his side, not noticing the blood stains on her lovely dress.

The critically injured man whispered something. She bent down to his face, reassuring him that she was nearby, but could barely understand what he tried to say. She bent closer to his lips. "Jesse," he whispered.

Doctor Goodfellow was said to be one of the best surgeons around and had treated numerous gunshot wounds in the rowdy town of Tombstone. The surgery seemed to last endless hours, and Lorraine assisted him as best she could. Finally, Doc Goodfellow caught the lead bullet in the end of a long pair of tweezers and dropped it with a loud clang into the tin bowl next to the table.

After he bandaged the wound, Goodfellow considered Cotton Joe's chances of survival at less than thirty percent. Lorraine stayed by the injured man's side for hours and prayed for her friend.

So far, there was no trace of Jesse Connor, and she tumbled between worry for him and confusion as to why he wasn't with Cotton Joe. "What in the world happened out there?" she mumbled to herself.

They must have been robbed at the mine. That was the only conclusion she came up with at the moment. She decided to ride out to her mine with Judge Taylor the very next morning. Maybe they would discover Jesse's whereabouts.

She barely slept that night and went over to the judge's house in the early morning. When they arrived at the mine, it was closed and locked up just like it was supposed to be.

"Strange," said Taylor. "Obviously they weren't robbed, at least not here. Was Cotton Joe carrying any silver on him when you found him unconscious in the wagon?"

Lorraine shook her head. *Why the hell had Jesse disappeared and not tended to his wounded partner?* The young feller was nowhere to be seen around town. *Who shot Cotton Joe? What had he meant when he whispered Jesse's name?*

Lorraine started to wonder if Jesse had betrayed her trust. He knew about the gold in the mine now. Usually Joe brought back the extracted gold from the daily shift since it was too risky to leave it in the mine. But there hadn't been any silver or gold on her poor friend's body. The leather pouch he normally wore under his shirt was gone and so was her other prospector, Jesse.

What if he shot Cotton Joe? The confused, dark-haired beauty shook her head. *Jesse wouldn't do such an evil thing ... or would he? He wasn't the same since that break up with his wife a few days back.*

A dark cloud of suspicion engulfed Lorraine's heart, fed by the flame of distrust. She had to find Jesse. And if she should discover that he had anything to do with the ambush, or that he had indeed shot his own partner, she would make sure he ended up on the gallows, no matter how she might have felt for him.

But she prayed to God she was wrong and that her instincts about Jesse when she first had hired him hadn't betrayed her. "You know Richard, if Jesse didn't have anything to do with the bushwhacking, he is probably dead as a door nail by now."

The judge nodded in agreement. Deeply concerned, she turned her horse around and rode back toward Tombstone. Judge Taylor followed her in silence, sensing her fear and discomfort. He knew how much Lorraine cared for Cotton Joe. The poor man had survived the surgery, but still battled for his life.

***

Jesse was alone in silence. Wild Linc must have left the old shack. The ground under him was hard, and his head ached. His swollen tongue filled his mouth, his stomach roiled, and he was desperately thirsty.

He tried to get up, but his hands were tied behind his back with a thin rope that cut into his wrists, and his feet were bound, making it difficult to stand.

Jesse was deeply worried about Joe and wondered if his friend had survived the gunshot wound. Probably not. Jesse didn't understand what he had gotten himself into, but then he recalled the words Wild Linc spit into his face about "stealing Lorraine." He whispered into the dark. "This is all about Lorraine."

That Duncan fellow had this crazy idea that he had rights to Lorraine, and that he, Jesse was somehow in the way. So Wild Linc must be the one who's been harassing her lately. That guy was obviously an obsessed and dangerous man. Picturing Lorraine in the arms of such a monster was unbearable for Jesse. "What a disgusting thought," he moaned. It made him sicker to his stomach and increased the pain of his injury.

The prisoner closed his eyes and tried to ignore the hammering headache. He worried that Lorraine would believe the lies Linc would tell her about Jesse shooting his friend. Hopefully not. He cared too much for Cotton Joe. *I would never harm Joe in any way, and I hope Lorraine knows that.*

Jesse would protect his partner with his own life. However, the young miner recalled the morning when Lorraine and Joe filled him in with the truth about the gold vein. The ambush was perfectly timed, and it would be easy for Lorraine to believe that he had gotten greedy over the gold. *For land's sake, I really hope I can convince her that I'm innocent. If I ever see her again, that is.*

Hell, he had to find a way out of this shack. It was vital for him to get out of this prison. Somehow, he had to escape and talk to Lorraine alone, to convince her he hadn't shot

Cotton Joe, and to prove Wild Linc was behind it all. But he had no idea how long Wild Linc would be gone.

Jesse worked at the ropes binding his wrists. They loosened a bit, but not enough to free himself. He teetered to his feet and hopped around the tiny room. After a while, he found a sharp edge on the backside of the shack wall. He rubbed the rope back and forth against it, gritting his teeth against the shooting pain in his arms. It didn't take long before his hands were full of splinters and his shoulders ached from being held in an awkward position. But he managed to further loosen the rope around his wrists.

He was furious at Wild Linc for shooting his friend like a dog, and trying to place the blame for the ambush on him. He growled at the empty room. "I swear to God, I am going to kill that bastard with my own hands!"

Anger rushed through him, and Jesse pulled like a madman against his bonds. The many weeks of chiseling in the mine finally paid off. His arm muscles bulged, and the weakened ropes shredded.

The sudden change in the position of his shoulders zapped through his torso like a lightning bolt, and the steady throbbing pain that followed made it difficult to move his arms. Jesse rubbed his numb wrists and hands. It hurt as the blood circulated through them again, but he had no time to feel sorry for himself.

"Quick, hurry up and get the hell out of here," he mumbled, forcing himself to move. He kicked hard at the wooden boards of the shed. Jesse wasn't sure what kind of building he was locked in, but he knew he had to escape as quickly as possible. He hoped that Wild Linc was far enough away so he wouldn't hear the commotion.

He kicked frantically at the old wooden wall like a wild stallion until some nails gave way, and two boards broke with a loud snap. It sounded as loud as a gunshot, and Jesse prayed that Lincoln Duncan hadn't heard it.

The opening was big enough and offered a way to freedom. Jesse squeezed himself through, ripping his shirt. He paid no mind to the damaged cloth, but chose a direction and ran. He didn't know where he was, running as fast as he could despite the thundering headache from the butt of the rifle. Fighting down nausea with each step, he hoped he could keep up the pace.

Finally, there was an area that looked familiar. A line of cottonwood trees ahead suggested he might not be far from the San Pedro River. The fleeing man stopped for a break, hiding behind a boulder, and he tried to catch his breath. Jesse was thirsty and exhausted—his pulse echoing like a steady drumbeat in his head, his heart pounding in his chest. He had no weapon to defend himself and no idea how to convince Lorraine of his innocence.

For one desperate moment, he was so overwhelmed that he considered fleeing the territory for good. It would be much safer than returning to Tombstone where the sheriff had most likely gathered a posse to search for him. Wild Linc must have poisoned the townsfolk's hearts by now.

But Jesse knew he couldn't run away and shook his head in disgust at the thought. He was a man of integrity and honesty. "I'll return to town to defend myself. I am not guilty." Plus, he hadn't forgotten about his hard-earned money stacked in the town's bank.

We shall see, Lincoln Duncan, who is the stronger man. In all my born days I never met such a cutthroat. I'll make sure you go to hell for what you did to my friend.

He didn't care much about what the townsfolk thought of him, but it was important that Lorraine didn't get the wrong image of him. She had been generous and helpful and deserved to know the truth.

So, he scrambled to his feet and walked toward the cottonwoods. When he arrived at the banks of the San Pedro River it was nearly dark, but he tried to go on a bit farther in hopes of throwing off Duncan off his trail in case the outlaw had discovered Jesse's escape and was tracking him.

The tired escapee dropped to his knees. He drank thirstily and cooled his head wound from the strike of the Winchester's stock. He winced as he touched the tender spot with his wet scarf. He dunked the bandana and wrapped it around his temples to soothe the throbbing headache. After resting a few minutes, Jesse crossed the river and continued his march through the scrub.

He heard the branches cracking, and Jesse stood still as a stone to listen. He assumed a crouching position behind a tree trunk, trying to determine if someone followed him. His heart beat rapidly. Fear that the highwaymen had already overtaken him gripped his chest. The guy who hated him had a horse and Jesse fled on his still-wobbly legs.

He listened to every sound and waited like a stone statue in the scrub. Abruptly a burro broke through the branches and gawked at him with huge dark eyes. Maybe the animal had escaped from one of the mines. Relieved and feeling a bit silly, Jesse exhaled.

"Trying to hide from people, too, are you?" The donkey snorted then moved forward and licked Jesse's hand which made him smile.

"You'd better make sure they don't catch you, my furry, gray friend."

As if the donkey understood, he turned and walked deeper into the brush. *Should I have caught the burro to use for riding into town? No, it will be easier to sneak quietly into Tombstone on foot.*

Again, the prospector looked through the brush and waited a few minutes before he dared move again. It seemed that the poor animal was really wandering around alone. He hoped the coyotes or cougars wouldn't grab his four-legged friend. For some reason he had always liked donkeys, and this one was a really cute burro with a white star on his forehead.

"Lord, forgive me, but I am dead tired and need to rest somewhere. I just can't walk anymore. Gosh, this headache is killing me."

Jesse stumbled through a dried-out wash next to the river bed and saw an old crumbling building. Three adobe walls still stood, but the roof was gone. Jesse pondered momentarily whether it was wise to hide in the ruins, but his tired body gave him the answer. He needed to get some sleep and those walls offered some protection.

"Lord, don't let me run into a snake or scorpion." He beat a branch against the adobe walls to ensure that all the critters abandoned the place for the night. Finally, Jesse sat carefully on the ground and leaned his back against a part of the wall that still held some of the day's warmth. He kept his boots on and, despite the very uncomfortable accommodation, fell asleep immediately. It was a shallow slumber haunted by bad dreams about Cotton Joe lying in his own blood and Wild Linc wearing a devil's mask.

CHAPTER EIGHTEEN

***

Jesse woke a few hours before daylight and staggered forward on his feet. He felt as if he had been run over by a stagecoach but moved back to the banks of the San Pedro.

Shambling along the shallow flow, he reached the little settlement of Fairbanks, a small mining community near Tombstone. It was crucial to avoid being seen, so he cut to the right and used the hills around the settlement to hide his approach to the town of Tombstone.

The risk of getting caught was high. Jesse tried to stay away from encounters with others but the closer he got to Tombstone, the more difficult that became. His progress was slow, and the hours went by quickly. By the time the exhausted man was close to the town limits, it was already late afternoon, and he decided to wait in an abandoned shaft until it was dark enough to walk to Lorraine's house. Fortunately, her home was at the edge of town and he hoped he would get there without being seen.

God, I hope she listens to me. She has to believe me! Jesse sat inside the entrance of the deserted mining shaft considering how to tell Lorraine the truth.

As the sun set in glorious colors, he stepped out of the abandoned mine. His cautious steps brought him to her white Victorian house. It was darkening rapidly, and this time Jesse was thankful for it. Striding confidently, he tried not to attract any suspicious glances in his direction.

Jesse was relieved to see a warm glow through the lace curtains of Lorraine's living room. He peeked through the window to see if she was alone, and spotted her sitting in a rocking chair, reading a book. A warm, cozy blanket lay across her lap. Lorraine looked lovely, and the scene so peaceful that it caused a stab of pain in Jesse's heart. He was scared that his appearance would permanently destroy that peaceful image in a few minutes' time.

Feeling devastated that events had taken such an ugly turn for Cotton Joe, Lorraine, and him because of that sick degenerate chasing her, he waited a moment longer, uncertain whether he should knock on the front door. *Wild Linc has messed everything up. My ungrateful wife, too. Oh, how I hate them both. I wish them dead. May God forgive me, but they don't deserve to live!*

Jesse did his best to shake off the appalling thoughts. He needed to remain calm and convince Lorraine that he didn't have anything to do with the shooting. Above all, he needed to assure her that he was worthy of her trust.

When the young miner knocked at the front door, he was shaking like a leaf during a breezy day. She came to the door and opened it a small crack. Her eyes grew huge when she recognized him. But before she could say anything or even scream, he quickly placed his index finger to his lips, and ushered her inside.

Obviously, she was surprised to see him at her house, but didn't hesitate and stepped back, holding the door open for him. He quickly came in and leaned against the closed door for a moment, trying to get his emotions under control.

She stared at him, and he realized how pale her delicate face was. At last Lorraine found her voice. "Where have you been, you bastard? Why weren't you with Cotton Joe when he was shot? What are you doing here?"

Jesse slowly raised his hands. "Lorraine, I beg you to listen to me! Please! I didn't have anything to do with Cotton Joe getting shot. We were on our way back from the mine when they jumped us."

"You mean someone robbed you?" Her arms crossed over her chest, and she clearly expected answers.

God, did she have to look so beautiful?

Jesse swallowed hard. "Listen, I don't know how much time I have to explain myself before they find me." He ran his fingers through his hair.

Lorraine was apprehensive about what he might say, and had a gut feeling she wouldn't like it at all.

"We were attacked by Wild Linc and two other outlaws."

"Wild Linc!—"

Jesse interrupted. "I know it sounds incredible, but please, just listen until I'm finished telling my side of the story. Then you can decide whether to believe me or not."

She closed her mouth and remained silent.

"He shot Cotton Joe without warning, but it wasn't a robbery. He held me prisoner and wants to pin the murder on me so that you'll hate me and want me hanged."

An exasperated sound came from her, and she angrily shook him.

"That is the biggest bit of balderdash I have ever heard. Lincoln might not be the most honorable man in town but why in the world should he even be interested in you unless he wanted to steal the silver? I don't believe a single word you say. For Lord's sake, I thought you were a man to ride the river with and now I find out you're nothing but a coward and liar."

Her words cut through him like sharp shards of glass and tried his patience bitterly.

"Lorraine, that curly wolf is obsessed with you. He sees me as competition. I have no notion how he got that idea but I am telling the truth. Linc Duncan knocked me unconscious and wants to blame me for killing your friend. Our friend. I managed to escape the shack where he kept me locked up and can show you the place. I'm sure I can find it again. For land's sake, part of my shirt is still hanging from the wooden boards I had to break through to escape. The other two outlaws are on their way to Mexico after he paid them. I'm telling the truth. Look at my head, this is where he knocked me off the wagon with his rifle."

He turned and she saw an ugly wound and his hair matted in dried blood. *My God, was it really possible or had Cotton Joe hit Jesse in self-defense?* She didn't know what to believe anymore. *I never felt so insecure in all my living days.*

Jesse saw the turmoil of her thoughts reflected on her face. "Cotton Joe, is he dead?" he asked carefully and feared the answer more than anything else at that moment.

"No, he is clinging to life for the time being but he is …"

The confused woman was just about to finish the sentence when she heard someone yelling her name in front of the house. "My God, it's Wild Linc!"

Panic rushed through Jesse's veins. He wouldn't have enough time to explain himself to her. They would surely arrest him now and probably hang him right away without trial

Lorraine stared into the face of the man standing in her living room. What should she do? Believe him? The story sounded too unreal. It would be safer to get him arrested right away.

"Lorraine, open the dang door. I need to talk to you!"

Wild Linc's rude voice and behavior brought her back to reality like a cold bucket of water tossed over her head.

She grasped Jesse's arm and pulled him to the room on the other side of the parlor.

"Quick, hide in there and don't make a sound. I'll handle this myself."

"Lorraine, be careful please. That man is really dangerous," Jesse whispered.

She nodded, then closed the door behind him. Heading to the front door, she tried to appear confident as usual.

"Lincoln, what the world is the matter with you? What's all this commotion about at this late hour? I'll not come to the saloon tonight, so go away and meet me another evening! I heard you found enough company among the French shady ladies lately!"

Wild Linc stomped past her, forcing entry into the house. He didn't respond to her remark about his adventure with the Frenchies. Lorraine was nervous that he was inside her private sanctuary.

"You know what, Lorraine? Your friend Jesse Connor is the one who shot Cotton Joe to rob him. He's a cold-blooded murderer! I caught him but, unfortunately, he escaped. That's enough proof that he's guilty, otherwise why would he run before standing trial? No, I tell you, girl, that worthless chap has betrayed not only Cotton Joe's trust, but yours as well. He needs to be arrested. Let's organize a posse to search for him, and then he'll get what he deserves—a California collar around his neck."

Lorraine stared at Wild Linc. *My word, he's full of hate for Jesse! But who tells the lies and who states the truth? I have to set a trap.*

Lorraine looked Wild Linc in the face. "You said he wanted to rob Cotton Joe and the mine? How would you know about that, and how come you were there to catch him? Seems like you were in the right spot at the right time."

Wild Linc was thrilled that his plan apparently was working, and was Lorraine starting to believe him.

"I happened to be out there hunting and heard the gunshot. You got that right. I was at the right place at the right time. I had him confessing and admitting that he wanted to rob the mine's yield and ride off with it. He must have felt pretty confident."

"So, you say you caught him at the mine?"

"Yes, my darling. He shot Cotton Joe right there at the gate. Poor chap, didn't even have time to lock it. Before I could do something for Cotton Joe, the horses took off, spooked by the gunshot."

Lorraine smiled sweetly at Wild Linc, and said, "My goodness, looks like you are a true hero, Linc. Well, go to the Oriental Saloon and wait there for me. I really have to reward you for taking the risk to catch such a dangerous outlaw. We'll organize a posse first thing tomorrow morning to hunt him down."

Duncan stared at her, surprised at the sudden charm she showed him. His feverish desire for her bubbled to the top and he licked his lips.

"Don't take too long, my beautiful bird."

She promised she would hurry and closed the front door behind him Leaning against it, she was shaky and frightened. The door to the other room opened slowly and Jesse stood in the door frame, waiting. His face was quite pale.

He had followed the whole conversation and didn't

understand why she had been so friendly to the outlaw at the end. Did she really care for him? Believe his lies?

Lorraine gently touched his head wound. He winced as the spot still hurt badly. Then a fact she had previously mentioned jolted him.

"Cotton Joe isn't dead, you said?"

She shook her head and her lush hair brushed across her shoulders.

"No, but he's in very serious condition. He might still survive, but the Doc's not sure yet. It's all in God's hands. All we can do is hope and pray. The doctor removed the bullet."

Jesse sank into one of the antique chairs. He had to digest the fact that his friend might not survive. Exhaustion and fear took its toll.

"So, do you believe my story or not?"

She stared into his eyes and said, "Yes."

"Why?"

She turned and looked out into the darkness.

"He said the shooting happened at the mine and that the gate wasn't locked. I was out there with Judge Taylor yesterday, trying to find out what happened. The gate was locked with Cotton Joe's padlock. There was no trace of damage or shooting at the mine. Everything was normal, no bullet shells, no blood. I knew you left the mine just like every day. He lied."

"But then, why are you still willing to meet with him?" Jesse looked at her with a puzzled expression.

"Nobody would believe you, so we need to set a trap with other witnesses to make sure we can prove that Wild Linc was the one who shot Cotton Joe and held you captive."

Dang, she was right. *But how can we convince the*

townsfolk? As Jesse looked at her attractive face, a small smile touched her lips.

"What is it?"

She slowly nodded.

"I know how we can catch him. I'll set a trap he can't resist. You stay here, and don't go anywhere. We mustn't let Wild Linc see you. I'll inform the judge and marshal first and then I'll meet with that ruthless monster."

Jesse didn't like it at all. He feared for Lorraine's safety more than ever. "Lorraine, if this goes wrong, chances are good that Wild Linc will attempt to harm you. He is cold-blooded and unpredictable."

She saw the fear in his eyes and came closer to hug him goodbye. It was a strange feeling for him to hold her in his strong arms, yet his heart beat much faster. Her scent caressed his senses.

When she was about to pull away to leave for Judge Taylor's house, he drew her back. His face bore a daring "now or never" expression as he bent down to kiss this amazing woman. Her lips were soft, and she was surprised by his move, but she gave in and kissed him back passionately.

It swept them away, and when they at last let go of each other, their eyes were filled with desire and their hearts knew that nothing would be the same after that kiss.

CHAPTER NINETEEN

***

Lorraine gathered her things and left the house. She still felt shaky and her legs were a bit wobbly. She had kissed many men but never had they affected her like this. *You better hold yourself together, woman. You have a dangerous task ahead.* She rushed to Judge Taylor's house to inform him of the latest development.

A few minutes later the judge left his home and went straight to the marshal's office. His face was grim. "Marshal, this is a very serious and dangerous situation. We cannot afford to make any mistakes now".

When the queen of the red-light district finally entered the poker section of the saloon, Wild Linc was already engaged in a game, and a half-empty glass of whiskey stood on the table next to his poker hand. He watched Lorraine walking toward the table, and waved her over.

"Come here, pretty bird. You might bring me some good luck for this game," he yelled and rudely yanked her onto his lap. His companions at the table laughed.

Sometimes Lorraine was surprised at the man's strength. *I wish I could stab you, you dirty, lying bastard,* she thought.

It took all of her self-control to remain charming and calm, at least for the moment. She had no intention of standing trial for killing him. He wasn't worth it, but she would see that justice got the better of him.

Lorraine kissed Linc and whispered that she would love to have a glass of champagne.

Surprised, he asked, "What's the matter? Do we have a reason to celebrate?"

She laughed, her voice ringing like a clear bell.

"Yes, indeed, my dear. First of all, you are a true hero it seems, and secondly, I got news from the doctor before I came here. That's why I was a bit late to meet you, my darling."

"What news?" he asked, squinting suspiciously.

"Guess what? Cotton Joe is much better. He's not unconscious any longer and can even talk. Tomorrow we can question him and then we'll set up the posse to hunt down that coward Jesse Connor. After all, we'll have two witnesses, and he'll have to stand trial for bushwhacking my friend."

She smiled sweetly at Lincoln Duncan, but he grew nervous the instant he heard the news and overlooked the fact that her smile didn't reach her eyes. Her eyes glittered cold, with barely hidden anger.

"Well, darling, how about some private time in the crib? You really deserve it. Won't charge you today, my brave Canadian lion!" she winked at him with a dazzling smile. But Wild Linc suddenly shoved her off his lap.

"Not tonight, my little dove. I don't feel well. Must have eaten something bad. I think I'd better call it a day and try to rest at home."

"Should I get you soup or something else?" Lorraine played the role of the concerned lover perfectly. But Linc shook his head. He dropped the cards and left the Oriental Saloon, obviously in a hurry to go home. He rushed through the darkness toward Toughnut Street.

Lorraine watched him from the entrance of the Oriental. She knew that Toughnut Street was a back route to Doctor Goodfellow's house and surgery and not to Linc's home.

She hoped and prayed that everything would work according to the plan the judge helped her set up. The lives of two close friends, as well as her mining business, were at stake. They took a big risk with this dangerous plot that could either be a great success or totally backfire.

***

The street around Doctor Goodfellow's house was dark and empty. "Good, don't need no bloody witnesses," a nervous Wild Linc mumbled under his breath. He knew that his life wasn't worth a plug nickel if the truth about the shooting and attack on the two miners became known in Tombstone. He had to take action as quickly as possible.

What Lorraine had announced as good news was a disaster for him. Not only would he lose the woman he desired if she found out the truth, but also probably end up with a noose around his neck for attempted double murder. *Oh well, I'd better make sure that Cotton Joe can't reveal any of the actual facts.*

He sneaked through the darkness to the backside of the doctor's house. Linc knew there was an extra room for hospitalizations at the rear of the Victorian home.

If he remembered right, there was a window which could be pushed open to grant him undetected entry. Linc had been in that room himself over a year ago while being treated for a minor wound caused by the knife of another gambler, so he knew the house like his own pocket. Slowly, carefully watching his steps, he walked to the window at the backside of the small building. The house lay in silent darkness. The town knew the upstairs apartment as the doctor's quarters where he was probably sleeping.

Wild Linc took a knife from his belt and carefully slid the blade between the window and sash to unlock it. It didn't take long before he was able to yank it open, producing a tiny creak. The dangerous man stood perfectly still, wondering if the noise had been heard inside the house. He waited patiently. The minutes passed but no lamp was lit and no sound came from upstairs so he carefully pushed the window all the way up in its weathered frame.

The room was dark and stale, warm air escaping through the window. Wild Linc carefully set a knee on the window-sill and pulled himself up. His sporty, lean figure made it easy. His boots scraped slightly over the outside wall but he did his best to avoid noise. Again, the gambler held his position and waited, crouched outside on the window's frame like a cougar ready to strike.

Linc Duncan had to make sure nobody heard him breaking into the doctor's home. Everything remained silent so he climbed through the opening into the room. It took some time until his eyes could discern outlines in the chamber. A three-quarter moon shined its pale light through the lace curtain, illuminating the chamber. Wild Linc was able to make out the bed where a figure lay under the covers, breathing shallowly but regularly.

For a moment the assassin considered using his knife but he didn't want to leave any trace. No, Cotton Joe had to die of natural causes. After all, he was badly injured so it was possible that he might worsen during the night and pass away in his sleep. The scamp Linc thought about it for a minute. *Ah, I found the perfect idea.* He slowly moved closer to the bed, a cruel smile on his face.

"Sleep, you fool, you'll never see daylight again," he whispered as he picked up a small pillow at the side of the bed. *Dang, the guy should have been dead since he fell off the seat of the wagon. I wonder how he's survived this long. Oh well, I am about to change that once and for all.*

The man under the sheets breathed calmly, the chest under the cover rising and falling in a steady rhythm, seemingly drifting in deep slumber. The outlaw raised the pillow and brought it down with one swift movement where he assumed Cotton Joe's face was. The man under the covers struggled with the pillow, kicking with his legs but the merciless outlaw held the pillow firmly onto the face hidden in the darkness.

"Drop it!" The voice was rough and cold as steel. Wild Linc felt a six-shooter at his temple and stood, frozen in shock. *What the hell ...* had Doc Goodfellow heard him?

The flame of an oil lamp flared, and the sudden source of light forced Linc to shut his eyes for a brief moment. The person under the pillow moved. The ruthless killer was shocked to see that it was Judge Taylor. *For heaven's sake, he had tried to murder a representative of the law. Why is the judge and not Cotton Joe under those dang covers? How could that be? The judge wasn't sick, or was he?*

Then it struck him like lightning. A trap, they had set up a trap. *That Connor guy must have found a way to inform and convince the judge and the doctor, that he was the one who had carried out the ambush.* Lincoln knew that the attempted murder of a territorial judge in front of a witness would require that he die on the gallows.

There was no way out now. For the first time in his life, Wild Linc was scared. The guy who held the Colt against his head was nobody else but Marshal White.

"Duncan, you are nailed to the counter! Let's move. There's a prison cell with your name on it until you stand trial. Judge, go ahead and take his gun and knife!"

Judge Taylor did as instructed, still red in the face and panting hard, struggling to catch his breath. When the prisoner and the marshal turned around, they saw Lorraine standing in the door frame.

The arrested man was shocked to see her but then he understood. *She knew about the trap. That was the reason why she had been so seductive at the saloon.*

Rage and hatred rushed through his veins like burning fire. "Damn you, Lorraine Bernard!"

After all, it was her fault that he had tried to kill Cotton Joe. She was the one who tricked him into his downfall tonight by feeding him false information. His burning desire turned into a wild flame of pure hatred.

"You! You set me up. You are nothing but a dirty, rotten Hell's Belle. You should have been happy and felt honored that I considered you as my legal wife. I could've had any of the other girls in town. You think you're something special, but you're not. I hate you, Lorraine, you hear me? I hate you! If I ever get a chance to escape the calaboose, I'll send you straight to Boot Hill, I swear! You'll go to hell with me, if it's the last thing I do!"

Marshal White pushed him forward.

"Pull in your horns. You've done enough talking, you dirty bastard. You are not in a position to threaten anyone around here anymore."

Wild Linc cursed all the way to the pokey and continued to yell profanities at Lorraine.

The door to the other room in Doctor Goodfellow's home opened, and Jesse Connor entered the room, the color drained from his face.

He was glad that the scum was arrested, but he was also deeply worried about Duncan's threats against Lorraine. *That outlaw meant every single word.* And Jesse knew that Duncan was cold-blooded. If he ever got the chance, he would surely try to kill Lorraine for setting him up.

"Where's Cotton Joe?" he asked Doctor Goodfellow, who pointed upstairs.

"We moved him to a safer room. He's still unconscious, but the fever is much lower. His chances of survival are actually increasing."

Jesse was thrilled to hear that. He would be devastated if he lost his friend. Yes, Cotton Joe had become a true companion and Jesse treasured their friendship.

Soon they all left Doctor Goodfellow's house. The judge went to his place, but not before asking Lorraine if she'd like to join him. Jesse didn't dare wait for her answer. The events of the evening had been confusing enough. He turned and walked away.

Lorraine thanked the judge for taking the risk of playing the decoy. "Honestly, the turmoil of this evening's events have exhausted me. I prefer to be alone in my own place tonight" Lorraine said.

The judge looked worried as he glanced toward the marshal's office where the criminal was locked up. He reassured himself that the marshal and his deputies would keep that monster behind bars until time for the trial. Judge Taylor hugged her briefly and wished her a peaceful night. He didn't want to admit that the attempted assassination had left him exhausted and shaken, too.

CHAPTER TWENTY

***

Lovely Lorraine, pale and upset after the night's ordeal, walked slowly home. She was tired to the bone, but too nervous for sleep. Sitting in her favorite rocking chair, she tried to read but couldn't concentrate on her book. She replaced it on the small table. The evening's events had left her in an emotional turmoil.

Seeing Jesse again, feeling distrustful toward him, then the kiss—remembering it still triggered butterflies in her stomach … all of it had been overwhelming. *Oh Lord, that pure hatred in Linc's eyes when he was caught.*

Lorraine paced back and forth, restless and confused. She had always felt safe and relaxed in her home, but now the walls seemed to close in around her. *If Linc ever escapes he would surely try to kill me.* That thought left her trembling.

The only thing that made her smile was the fact that Cotton Joe was indeed getting a bit better. "I sure am grateful that Jesse is innocent and hasn't betrayed my trust," she whispered into the empty living room.

She went to her bedroom and dressed in her nightgown,

wrapping a cozy shawl around her shoulders. A cup of freshly brewed tea stood on a small table but she hadn't touched it. Rocking back and forth in her chair, trying again to read about mining methods, she nearly jumped at the sound of a knock at the door. Scared to open it, Lorraine grasped a derringer she kept in the drawer next to her bed. Walking slowly to the door, she hesitated to open it, her heart pounding against her ribcage.

"Who is it?" She asked through the closed door.

After Wild Linc's cursing and threats against her, she had to be careful.

"It's me, Jesse!"

Astonished, she unlocked the entry while holding the ends of her shawl together at her chest. He stared at her.

"I know it's not the best time and you're probably preparing for bed, but I wonder if you'd allow me to come in for a few minutes."

She stepped back and looked into his pale face. "Why are you here, Jesse? As you can see, I'm really not prepared for a visitor."

My God, I must sound ridiculous. Me, a soiled dove complaining about not being decently dressed for a male visitor. He glanced around the room and not at her.

"I was on my way home, but I can't settle down. There's no way I'd be able to sleep now. To be honest, I was worried about that Duncan fellow and his threats against you." He ran his fingers through his hair, feeling confused.

"Jesse, I'll be fine. Linc's in jail now."

He nodded. "To be honest I don't even know why I've knocked at your door." He turned away as if to leave again. *God, I could use a stiff drink, or better yet, two.* But he hesitated, door knob in his hand. There was something he needed to tell her and if he didn't do it now, he would probably never again have the guts to do so.

"I should feel guilty about that kiss I gave you, you being my employer and involved with Judge Taylor and all. But as a matter of fact, Lorraine, I don't regret it. And I didn't kiss the Scarlet Queen. I kissed you, the woman I desire. That's all I wanted to tell you. I wish you a good night's rest, Miss Bernard."

His confession took her by surprise. She didn't know what to say and nodded.

"You know, I'm aware that you hired me and you're my boss. But I'm not one of your customers. When I kissed you, I did so because I wanted to, because I have feelings for you as a woman. I am pining away for the strong in-credible person you are.

"I have never seen you as a lady of easy virtue but as the friend who granted me a successful start in this God-forsaken town. I admit, I think you are quite a handful to handle, but, in my opinion, you are a hell of a woman and the best friend a person could ever have in their life. I'm a simple man, not rich. I'm not an impressive judge who could offer you a rosy future in a big mansion. I'm just me, Jesse Connor, a heartbroken man who earns his money with his hands, paid by a woman, and I don't even want to think about how she earns that money she pays me for my labor. I thought the worst thing in my life was the fact that my faithless wife left me. But God forgive me, the worst thing indeed is to want you and try to force my silly heart to remain silent."

She stared at him open-mouthed, unable to say a single word. Men had confessed their feelings to her before, but it had never touched her the way his words did now.

"I'm sorry, Jesse. Maybe I should have never hired you. I didn't mean to make you suffer." She turned away from him but he covered the distance with two steps of his long legs.

"Hush, don't you say another word, Lorraine Bernard!" His grip was like steel, his arm muscles bulged under his shirt, and his eyes were dark with fury and passion.

"You are lying to yourself. You and I both try to suppress feelings we can't fight much longer. At least have the backbone to admit it!"

Despite his aggressive stance, she wasn't afraid of him. Deep in her heart she knew he would never hurt her and believed he meant every word he said. *He's right. We can't deny our feelings for each other any longer. I am indeed lying to myself if I keep on pretending that I don't desire this man.*

He stared into her alluring, almond-shaped eyes. Her lips were open slightly, and he smelled a trace of her perfume. It was intoxicating. Her shawl slid to the ground, leaving the creamy curve of her full breasts visible. He saw the pulse beating rapidly at her neck.

"Lorraine, you'd better send me away, right now. Help me to resist this before I do something I might regret later."

She saw the turmoil reflected on his handsome features, but she shook her head. "I can't send you away. I would betray myself if I did."

He stared into her luminous green eyes and felt as if he were drowning in them. He bent down. More than anything in his life, he wanted to kiss this woman. And he did. And again. But not as carefully as the first time, hours ago.

This kiss was raw, hungry, passionate. He meant to be gentle but he was swept away by his own burning desire for this woman. His lips pressed on her softer ones. His tongue parted them, and he conquered her mouth with it.

Her tongue met his and a small sigh escaped her. Hearing it was enough for him to lose restraint. He dug his hand into her hair piled atop her head. How soft it felt.

His other hand rested on her waist. She felt his chest and arm muscles, hard as rock under his shirt. All the chiseling in the mine had created an extremely muscular torso. She couldn't resist touching him under his shirt, feeling the warmth of his skin. Tracing his skin with the tips of her fingers felt like touching one of those antique marble statues she had seen in the fancy houses on the east coast, yet his skin was warm and giving.

Heat rose in her body, and her heartbeat increased, hammering against her ribs. She was sure he must hear it beating. *My God, what's happening to me?*

She was confused by the emotions he triggered so easily in her.

I should send him home right now before this gets out of control. When she took an uncertain step away from him, he watched her. His eyes were full of desire, dark and smoldering.

He whispered, "You had a chance to send me away, my love, but it's too late now."

Jesse smiled that boyish smile she had liked so much from the very first time she saw him. She smiled back. Then she shrieked like a small girl as he easily lifted her and carried her into the adjoining room.

He gently placed her on the bed. The whole room smelled of Lorraine and he was aware that he was an intruder in her most private space. He kissed her again, carefully trying to avoid hurting her with his weight. But she pulled him close, and he knew she must feel the reaction the kiss had caused in his body. Surprisingly, her profession didn't enter his thoughts for one second.

This was Lorraine Bernard, the woman he had fallen

for, the woman he wanted with a desire he had never felt before. In that room she wasn't the singing Calico Queen from the Oriental Saloon, nor the shady lady. *This is the woman that drives me crazy, the one who touches this broken heart of mine. She put herself at risk for me at the French brothel when my own wedded wife let me down.*

Jesse slowly undressed her, admiring every inch of her ravishing body. She, who always was in charge and in control, gave in and didn't lead the game of love.

Lorraine saw his passion and feelings reflected in his eyes like a burning fire and every single touch of his spoke of respect and desire for her. Jesse Connor was one of a kind whom she would never compare to another man. She knew she had lost control and was falling for this man. For the first time she wasn't able to command her heart. Strangely, it seemed right, them being together. It felt as if she had always belonged to him.

Lorraine knew that love was a dangerous game that often led to heartache, but she didn't want to be anywhere else right now than in her lover's strong arms. Those arms that held her so tightly while his lips and hands explored every inch of her stunning body.

Jesse marveled at her beauty, the taste of her skin and the way she responded to his kisses and caresses. Every single moan, every sigh from her lips encouraged him and increased his hunger for her. When they finally united, it wasn't only physical, but their souls and hearts connected in that moment.

They made love to each other for hours until the pale morning light crawled through the window. She slept in his arms, and he silently watched her. Never had he experienced such a deep understanding and connection with a woman. Never had any female answered his needs with the same untamed hunger. He closed his eyes and whispered, "Please God, help me, I love this woman!"

She stirred slightly in his arms but slept on. The next thing Jesse knew was waking up to the tender touch of her warm hands moving over his naked body. He must have dozed off. Now he smiled at her.

"You are wearing me out, boss." But he rolled over and showed her that he still had enough strength and energy left to satisfy her hunger for him once again.

CHAPTER TWENTY-ONE

***

Two days later Doctor Goodfellow confirmed that Joe would survive his gunshot wound. Jesse promised Lorraine that he would continue working at the mine until Cotton Joe was well enough to prospect, if he wished to continue his mining job.

Lorraine didn't like the idea of Jesse working at the mine. She trusted him completely, but she knew the dangers of working alone underground. One of the mine shafts could collapse and bury him alive or trap him with limited oxygen. Now that she'd found him, Lorraine was afraid to lose him, and realized how complicated that would make life from now on. She wondered what he expected from her. *What if he wants me to give up my life as a lady of the night and doesn't accept me meeting other men? What should I tell the judge? Am I ready to settle down? I have achieved so much. Should I really give all that up to be with one single man?*

Lorraine had seen men come and go, and although Jesse was indeed special, she found it difficult to trust her feelings, or his for that matter.

Time will tell, but I need some space to reorganize my whole life. He would have to understand, or leave me. It's as easy as that. I am Lorraine Bernard, the most successful soiled dove in Tombstone.

Some called her the uncrowned Queen of the Fallen Angels. Wouldn't her star lose its shine if everyone knew she had settled for one man?

Jesse was on his way to the mine. The shock of the ambush still fresh in his memory set his nerves jangling. He peered behind every scrub and bolder. The young miner knew he had only survived because he escaped the shed. Cotton Joe's continued struggle for health stayed on his mind

With an extra Winchester in the wagon and a six-shooter in his holster, a worried expression clouded Jesse's face. After watering the team, he readied himself to enter the shaft.

Images of the night he had spent with Lorraine flooded his mind. He mumbled, "Dang, this woman is any man's dream. Thinking of her lips kissing me will probably distract me so terribly that I wouldn't be astonished if I hit my own hand with the hammer today."

The thought that she was the dream of many men in Tombstone triggered an unfamiliar jealousy. "What do you expect, you fool? That her past and profession would simply vanish into thin air? You better get yourself together, Hoss." He continued talking to himself while chiseling away in the mine tunnel.

No doubt about that Lorraine was a love goddess. but she was also a woman of ill fame. *How will I handle other men laying hands on her body if they pay enough money?*

Returning to town in the early evening, he visited Cotton Joe and Doctor Goodfellow. His friend was able to speak, but he was still weak. He pulled a chair closer to the bed and slowly told Joe the tale of the events following his shooting. Cotton Joe's eyes opened wide as he listened in alarm. When Jesse finished, Joe nodded.

"Good! The bastard's in the pokey now. I'll tell the judge how he gunned me down mercilessly as if I was a mad dog. We'll see him dangling from the gallows soon just like he deserves!"

Jesse nodded. Cotton Joe waited as he sensed there was more to it. When his young friend remained quiet, Cotton Joe closed his eyes for a moment. Then he spoke slowly. "It's Lorraine, isn't it? You've fallen for her, haven't you?"

Jesse was surprised. "How…?"

"How did I know? I've seen it growing since we went to her place for breakfast that day and picked up our pay. But that's not important now. Fact is, you know how she earns her money. If you're not able to handle that without jealousy, you'll have to forget about her. She needs a man who loves her with all her flaws and not a person who bosses or controls her. Lorraine Bernard belongs to nobody, Jesse! But if she gives you her heart she might come to her senses and settle down one day."

Jesse nodded. "I know that, Joe. But she has to decide that all by herself. I can't make her.

Joe continued, "Eventually she will, but only when she has the feeling the time is right for her to do so. Do you understand what I'm saying, Jesse? She's a fine woman but you have to be patient and wait. It'll takes time for her to trust enough to hand over her heart and make you part of her future. If she feels cornered, you'll lose her faster than you can hit a rock with a chisel."

Jesse knew Joe was right and promised to follow his advice. When he was about to leave, he turned and looked at his pale friend lying in bed.

"Joe, I thank God you're still alive. I'd sure miss you terribly as a friend and adviser if anything ever happened to you."

Cotton Joe nodded weakly then closed his eyes and went back to sleep. Jesse knew the man was exhausted and prayed he would completely recover from his injuries. He regretted deeply that he hadn't been able to protect Cotton Joe from getting shot.

Jesse pondered whether to go to Lorraine's place, but despite their passionate night together, uncertainty gripped him. Cotton Joe was right. It didn't make sense to stalk her or to try and control her. He had to wait and let destiny decide if they were meant to be together. So he took care of the horses and checked on Cotton Joe's cabin. Then he rode to his own house to try to find some rest. He had no food, but wasn't hungry anyway. He hit the bed and fell into a deep, dreamless sleep.

***

Miners, gamblers, and soiled doves crowded the saloons and brothels in town. "Ladies of the line" came from their tents in the mining camps for an evening inside. Lorraine tried to concentrate on the conversations around her but her thoughts returned to the handsome miner she had hired months ago, and who now was more than just an employee.

He hadn't appeared at her place after work, but she knew he'd visited Cotton Joe to check on his slow recovery. She was torn between disappointment and relief that he hadn't come to see her. Falling for the guy had left her in an emotional turmoil, especially after they'd made love.

Quite a few well-paying men tried to charm Lorraine into an adventurous night together. *I can't stand the thought of another man's hands on my body today. Not after experiencing Jesse the way I did that fateful evening.* She remained at the saloon entertaining a few guests at the poker table, occasionally singing a song.

The saloon owner never objected to whatever Lorraine wanted to do. Her presence alone increased the numbers of drinks sold. As the evening grew rowdier, and the guests got drunker and more dangerous to handle, she withdrew to her house.

As she walked home, her small gun hidden and loaded in her purse, she recalled the first evening Jesse had escorted her home. *I shouldn't feel like this, but I really miss the guy. It seems like ages ago when I first met him and he saw me home.*

***

On the other end of Allen Street, Marshal White checked on his prisoner again. Wild Linc appeared to be sleeping on the bunk in his cell. He had calmed down since the evening he was arrested. Boy, had he cursed all the people involved in setting the trap. The marshal took the threats he spit out seriously indeed.

Lincoln Duncan was known as a dangerous and ill-tempered man and surely wouldn't hesitate to commit murder. So far, none of the rumors about crimes he was supposed to have committed had been proven true. The marshal hoped it was different this time, and Wild Linc would be sentenced to the punishment he deserved. If the lawdog had a say, Wild Linc would meet justice at the town's gallows.

At first, Marshal White didn't hear the faint knock at the door, but he did the second time. He went over to see who it was. Probably someone trying to get him to intervene in some silly fight in one of the countless saloons.

Marshal White wished they would stop pumping whiskey twenty-four hours a day, seven days a week in this town. It fueled aggressive behavior among the already hard-to-handle miners, outlaws, cowboys, and women of ill-fame.

He was getting too old for this job and considered settling down on a small ranch. He planned to resign his position as lawman come spring. It was time for a younger fellow to handle all the lunatics who made Tombstone their home. He'd already told the town's leading men about his decision.

As the Marshal opened the door, he was surprised by two things: first, the trace of perfume drifting into the pokey from a well-known soiled dove named Blonde Mary and second, that a gun pointed right at his gut.

He slowly stepped backwards, not knowing what this was about, but something in the woman's eyes told him that she wouldn't hesitate to use her weapon. He didn't like the cruel smile she wore.

Blonde Mary entered the room and waved the gun toward the door of the cell. "The keys, Marshal!"

Marshal White was shocked to see she intended to free the prisoner. "Mary, this man is a mighty dangerous feller. Linc is locked away for attempted murder in three difference cases. God knows what other crimes he has committed. You shouldn't consider mingling with him."

"Well, lawdog! That is my business, I'd say. Would you now be so kind as to open the door for my man, or I'll have to shoot you right there where you stand!"

Meanwhile, Wild Linc had gotten off his bunk and stood waiting at the cell door, holding the iron bars. He was surprised that Blonde Mary was brave enough to free him from the calaboose. Looks like he left quite an impression on the woman during their few nights together. *She has more grit than I thought.*

Wild Linc grinned. Not that he really cared for her, but it sure came in handy right now that she wanted to spring him out. Her actions would probably save him from the hangman. Once he was able to escape, he could drop her any time. He had other plans as soon as he was free.

Marshal White hesitated but her weapon convinced him to unlock the door. The prisoner stepped out and Blonde Mary hugged him. He callously pushed her away and took the gun from her. Pointing it at the marshal, he ordered him to step into the cell. The only thing that saved the lawdog's life was the fact that a gunshot would have aroused too much attention from the people walking by, and Linc had no knife to kill him quietly.

The outlaw swiftly turned the gun with one fast movement of his right arm and knocked the marshal unconscious with the butt of the six-shooter. He locked the prison cell door, dropped the keys in the desk drawer, and sneaked out of the pokey followed by Blonde Mary. The marshal lay on the floor with blood seeping into his blond hair.

"Linc, we can hide you at my brothel if you want but I also have a horse saddled for you behind the building if you want to ride out of town. I think that would be safer. I've got some money saved up for you, too."

He smiled in a sinister way. "Well, well, I'll be darned. You are a decent woman after all, hmmm!" She smiled, soaking up his compliment like a flower bathing in the rays of the sun.

"Listen woman, I made some promises before I got arrested and have some open bills to settle with a few people here in town, so I'll hide for a few days. But then I'll come back to teach them a lesson about messing with Lincoln

Duncan! Until then, you'll keep me informed, Mary. I'll be hiding at the old cabin close to the fork of the trail that leads to Fort Bowie."

Blonde Mary eagerly nodded, and pointed to a dark gelding waiting behind the neighboring building.

"Quick, get out! The saddle bags are packed with food and there's a flask of whiskey as well."

"You did well, Mary." He leaned down and roughly kissed her, then jumped into the saddle and rode off. Blonde Mary smiled in the darkness, obviously proud about saving "her" man. Her plan had worked perfectly.

CHAPTER TWENTY-TWO

***

Lorraine lay awake in her bed and savored Jesse's scent still lingering between the sheets. She imagined his strong, warm body next to hers. *Unbelievable, I really miss him. It's lonely without his company.*

Outside town Jesse tossed and turned in his sleep. Neither of the lovers had the slightest idea about what had happened at the jail. Nobody knew that Wild Linc was free and preparing a rampage against those who had tried to get him hanged.

The next morning Jesse went to the mine early. Lorraine walked to the local seamstress to buy a new dress. In the midst of the fitting, the door flew open and the marshal's wife stomped into the store. She complained about men in general and her husband specifically, who had stayed out all night.

"Probably spent the night in the bed of one of those horrid, soiled women."

She stared hatefully in Lorraine's direction who pretended not to be paying any attention to the woman's rude words. She knew the marshal well enough to be convinced that he wasn't the kind of guy to stay in a brothel the whole night.

The man's absence struck her as odd. Finishing her dress fitting, Lorraine decided to check on the law man at his office. When she knocked, no one answered the door. The doorknob turned in her hand, and she entered. The marshal wasn't at his desk as she expected. She was about to leave when she heard a low moan.

Startled, took a few steps inside and was shocked to see the town's lawdog imprisoned in his own cell. Dried blood was clotted in his hair and left an ugly stain on the front of his shirt. He blinked at her and tried to stand. She saw him swaying with dizziness and ran over to him.

"The keys, marshal. Where are the keys?"

He pointed to his desk, and she yanked open each drawer until she found them. She tried all the keys, and the last one fit so she could unlock the cell door. The marshal tried to walk, but couldn't keep his balance. Wild Linc had dented his opponent's skull with the force of his blow.

Lorraine ran out to Allen Street and called for help. It didn't take long before men ran toward the jail and tended to the town's lawman. Someone rushed to fetch the doctor immediately. The marshal's wife came running, but she didn't dare look at Lorraine. She blushed with embarrassment about her false accusation at the dress shop and tried to tend to her husband.

Only then did it strike Lorraine like a bolt of lightning. *Wild Linc was gone! Sakes alive, the dangerous man was free.* The news of the outlaw's escape spread like wildfire, and Judge Taylor assembled a posse to find him. They rode out of town less than an hour later. A dozen men led by the marshal's brother and cousin were eager to hunt Linc Duncan down.

Down in the gold shaft chiseling away, Jesse knew nothing of this. He had decided to ignore the silver shaft for now and catch up on the loss of manpower as Cotton Joe recuperated. Finding more gold would earn more money for Lorraine. He knew that doctor bills would be coming soon. The sooner Cotton Joe recovered completely, the better.

When he was done for the day, he locked the gate and climbed onto the wagon. *It sure is lonely working out here without Joe.* When Jesse arrived back in town, Lorraine ran toward him. He yanked on the reins to slow the horses, knowing something was wrong, fearing it was Cotton Joe. He jumped off the wagon and pleaded with Lorraine, "Joe, is he …?"

He was afraid of her answer, but she shook her pretty head, gasping. He couldn't recall ever having seen her so upset.

"What is it, Lorraine?"

"Wild Linc escaped. The Marshal was hit on the head and can't tell us how. I assume someone helped him but we don't know who. They've searched the whole town. He's gone. Do you know what that means? Wild Linc will try to kill both of us."

He stood closer and embraced her. "Hush, my girl, I won't let anybody hurt you."

He tried to comfort her, but she pulled away from him, aware they were in the middle of Allen Street. She glanced around nervously, concerned that people might surmise how close she and Jesse were. When she pulled away, it him hurt him deeply. *She doesn't trust me or even worse, she doesn't want anybody to realize we're together.*

Jesse stared at her in disbelief, and she looked at the ground. She knew she had hurt him, but couldn't say anything right now. She had set a boundary and wouldn't allow herself to cross it. He waited but when she expressed no feelings for him, he shook his head.

"Here is today's yield from the mine. You can put that in the bank, ma'am."

Then he turned and walked away. She held the pouch in her small hand and stared after him.

"God, I'm a fool. I really hurt him," she murmured to herself. In that instant, she hated the gold in her hand. *I hate this town and I am disgusted by the thought of being a woman of easy virtue for the rest of my life.* Lorraine Bernard felt as if she had lost herself watching Jesse walking away from her toward the wagon. He didn't turn around once.

That evening Lorraine went to the Birdcage Theatre to visit to some of her friends among the shady ladies. She wasn't looking for entertainment but was simply afraid to be alone in her house. Remembering Wild Linc's threats, she didn't dare spend the night without company. "Jesse won't be there to shield you from harm. You chased him away, silly girl," she mumbled while entering the Birdcage.

Meanwhile, Lorraine's lover lay awake in his little house. He thought about her and their situation. *Lord, I know I have to give her up. Lorraine will never quit her life of prostitution for me. She proved that this afternoon. I should have never slept with her. Foolish enough to sleep with your boss woman. What were you thinking?*

He didn't know how to face her now and cursed himself for losing control in her bed. But when he thought back to that night, he yearned for her, and not only physically. *God, how I miss her.*

However, that night together seemed like ages ago. Jesse was worried. *How am I supposed to protect her from that mad Duncan when she is so distant with me?* The handsome miner was certain that Wild Linc wasn't only cold-blooded, but also insane and obsessed with Lorraine. No, he didn't like the situation at all. Jesse was sure that Wild Linc wouldn't give up on Lorraine so easily. He would most likely make sure no other man ever laid hands on her. "He will try to kill her. For Christ's sake, how am I gonna prevent that?" he asked into the dark room.

The posse returned late that night but hadn't found any trace of the fugitive. They intended to continue their search with the first daylight the following day.

Lorraine hoped they would catch the guy right away. Judge Taylor sent one of the deputies to keep an eye on her house. That comforted her some, but she knew Wild Linc was a sneaky sort, and might get around the guards.

The next morning Jesse decided not to go to the mine. He was convinced that Wild Linc was out for revenge and would most likely try to find an opportunity to catch the fallen angel alone without witnesses.

Jesse wasn't fooled easily. He knew the curly wolf wouldn't have many chances to come for them both, and would surely not waste his time on the judge or marshal who had set up the trap at the doctor's house. *No! Wild Linc would come for me because he sees me as a competitor, and for Lorraine because she has denied him her heart.*

The young prospector decided to hunt down the outlaw himself. The posse didn't seem to be efficient. They looked all over the county, but Jesse was certain that Wild Linc was hiding somewhere nearby so he could strike when least expected.

He wondered aloud, "Who is helping you in this town? Who is the traitor that freed you from the calaboose?" His horse listened to him talking to himself while he saddled the patient animal.

Jesse would try to protect Lorraine just as he had

promised, and once that task was fulfilled, he would leave Tombstone, and forget about the lucky strike and the home he had tried to build for his ex-wife.

"I need to forget Lorraine too," he mumbled. He was a man of his word and wouldn't let Wild Linc harm her. *The only thing I'll never achieve is conquering her heart.*

With a heavy heart he buckled his holster around his lean hips, took his shotgun and a water flask, and rode out on a deadly mission.

***

Lorraine hadn't slept well. She watched the posse ride out of town but wondered if Lincoln was really that far. Just like Jesse, she doubted he'd give up on revenge against her or her beloved miner. "There'd been too much hate in his eyes when he'd made his threats against us. Linc wouldn't simply run away. He'd look for a chance to get even with Jesse and me," she whispered.

The worried beauty carried her gun day and night now, and she slept with another six-shooter on the night stand. She knew her life was in danger but wasn't willing to let it scare her out of her mind. She had a business to run and money to earn.

Jesse hadn't picked up the wagon today and Lorraine wondered if she would need to look for another prospector for the mine in case he vamoosed. It was time to walk over to Doctor Goodfellow's home to pay a visit to Cotton Joe and to talk with him about his mining partner. Upon arrival, the doctor told her that Joe felt much better this morning and the he'd had some men take him to his cabin. "Oh, it's wonderful to hear that! At last some good news." She exclaimed.

She hurried uptown to the Birdcage Theatre where she

spoke to the owner. She promised to pay a considerable sum if he could spare one of the doormen who normally kept an eye on the rowdy guests of the premises, at least for a few days. Lorraine wanted to hire him temporarily to protect not only her house, but that of Cotton Joe's as well.

Hutchinson understood her wish and offered his help immediately as he was equally worried about the situation. He didn't want to lose the most desired lady of the night to some lunatic like Wild Linc. After all, Lorraine was well liked in the red-light district and no man would dare let her down.

Jesse patrolled the area around Tombstone looking for tracks or any other sign of Wild Linc. He decided to stay closer to his lover's house and the hills behind it. Sooner or later the culprit was bound to show up.

CHAPTER TWENTY-THREE

***

The last three nights had been restless. Jesse hardly slept, and exhaustion crept into his bones.

Meanwhile, Lorraine wondered about him, but wasn't surprised that she hadn't heard from him. *He must be furious with me.* As she sat in her rocking chair, Lorraine had no idea that Jesse was guarding her house from a distance behind the hill.

The Birdcage guard sat at his post outside before her door. It was late, well past midnight, and the calico queen had fallen asleep in the living room with a book in her lap. A rough hand covered her mouth, and she shrieked beneath it. A burly man pulled her roughly from the chair. When she tried to turn, she looked straight into Wild Linc's face. She saw a mask of pure hatred, his eyes glittering dangerously.

How in the world did he get into the house past the guard? Lincoln Duncan threw her across the room and she thudded into the opposite wall. The impact left her face and shoulder stunned with pain. *Good heavens, he's here to kill me. I have to fight for my life.*

"Try to run—you won't escape," he hissed at her. "That

feller outside won't hear you! I killed him dead as a door-nail, you hear me? And you will be, too pretty soon. But first, I'll enjoy that gorgeous body of yours one last time."

Lorraine gasped in horror. Linc yanked her around by the arm and sent her sprawling on the floor. Although she was strong, she was no match for him.

With his right hand closed around her throat, he forced his hips between her legs while trying to raise her skirt. She fought and kicked under him, and to her disgust, she realized it aroused him even more to choke her. He was completely out of control, like an animal. Lincoln Duncan had turned into a monster greedy for murder.

The room swirled around her and she felt lightheaded. His strong grip on her throat increased even as he continued tearing at her clothes. Lorraine pulled at his hand with both of her small ones. Now the room turned darker around her, and she felt weaker with each passing moment.

So, this is going to be it. Jesse, my handsome Jesse. I wish I had told you how much you mean to me. But she could no longer think. Lorraine fainted and went limp. Wild Linc tore open her dress. Blinded by his rage and desire for the unconscious woman on the floor, he paid no attention to his surroundings. His blood rushed through his body. Never in his entire life had he felt such intense lust, and he hated her even more than ever for commanding his male needs. As he was about to force himself onto her body a shotgun cracked inside the room.

The blast threw Wild Linc backward off her body and across the room. Blood splattered the wall in a grotesque pattern. White smoke filled the living room and the smell of black powder irritated the shooter's throat.

Wild Linc Duncan's legs kicked out a few times as blood soaked his dirty shirt. A wound gaped in his chest where the bullet found its deadly target. He tried to focus on the other side of the room, and saw a man stepping through the billowing gun smoke. But the wound was too grave for him to understand who had shot him.

Turning his gaze back to the unmoving woman on the floor, he uttered a hoarse sound, "Whore!" Then his head lolled slightly to the side. Life was over for Lincoln Duncan. The man known as Wild Linc among Tombstone's townsfolk was dead, his blood staining the wooden floor beneath him.

***

Jesse dropped the shotgun and ran over to Lorraine where she lay. She didn't move so he shook her gently, cradling her like a child in his strong arms. He thought it might help to blow air into her lungs, again and again. He wasn't willing to give up on her, and he forced his own breath into her mouth.

After hearing the gunshot, people came running to the house, gunning first for Jesse. They found the guard in front of the house. The blade of Lincoln's Bowie knife was buried all the way to the handle in the poor guy's guts. Then they saw Wild Linc lying dead on the floor, covered in his own blood.

The doctor rushed to Lorraine's side and asked Jesse what he thought he was doing breathing into her mouth. "For heaven's sake man. Give her some air."

"That's what I'm doing Doc. Air from my own lungs. He exhaled into Lorraine's mouth one more time."

Doctor Goodfellow begged, "Open your eyes, Lorraine, please. Look at me, Lorraine! For heaven's sake breathe, Woman!"

Suddenly she coughed and drew in a deep breath,

wincing at the pain in her throat. That cough was the sweetest sound to Jesse's ears. He laughed with tears rolling down his cheeks. Finger-shaped bruises already showed on the poor woman's neck and throat, but, thank God, she was alive.

"I would say that was a very close call. I reckon you saved her life, miner," Doctor Goodfellow said.

Lorraine was shaken, and she needed a few minutes to recall what had happened. When she saw Jesse, she clung to his shirt and tried to speak, but only a weak wheezing escaped her lips.

"You won't be able to talk for a few days, my dear. That guy almost squashed your throat through the back of your neck," Doctor Goodfellow explained. She nodded and Jesse lifted her.

"I'll bring her to Cotton Joe's cabin until this mess is cleaned up. I'll stay there, too, and keep an eye on both of them, Doc!"

"Very well then, I'll deliver some medicine to heal her throat and vocal cords first thing tomorrow. Got to change Cotton Joe's bandage anyway. However, I can't heal Lorraine's shock. It's a good thing she won't be alone tonight. You might as well give her a shot of whiskey."

Jesse carried the woman he loved so dearly over to Cotton Joe's home. Some of the men standing around went into her Victorian home and picked up the dead body of Wild Linc. They left a trail of still warm blood on the floor.

Cotton Joe was shocked when he learned what had happened. He felt helpless and frustrated that he hadn't been able to protect his dear friend himself and told them so. "I wasn't at her side when she most needed me." Joe felt guilty but was grateful that Jesse was around and would never forget that the young lad had saved Lorraine's life.

***

The next few days, the town's most popular fallen angel stayed put. She remained at Cotton Joe's cabin until workers cleaned up everything at her house. The judge had seen to it, and the wall in her living room sported beautiful, new wallpaper with a rose flower design.

But Lorraine couldn't help feeling scared being alone in her own house. The near-death experience had left her deeply frightened. In all her years as a lady of the night, she had never experienced such a brutal attack. *Heck, I don't even know if I can return to my trade.* She spent many hours at Cotton Joe's cabin, tending his wound and tending her throat while she thought calming thoughts. Cotton Joe spoke to her like a father to his child.

"Lorraine, we don't know if there will be a savior around if you are attacked again like this. Remember the girl you saved some time back? If you hadn't stabbed the fellow, she'd be dead now. This time you were very lucky because Jesse was watching your house. He's a man who'd give his own life for you and who loves you to the moon and back."

She opened her mouth to object but he raised his hand.

"Listen to me, I might be a quiet person and generally tend to my own business. But I'm not blind, and I like you both a hell of a lot. That Jesse Connor fellow is head over heels for you but in a different way than all the other fools in this rotten town. All he sees in you is the woman you are, not the soiled dove, not the owner of a mine, and surely not just a shapely body. You could be as poor as a church mouse or working in a laundry shack, and he wouldn't mind. That man was out there, protecting you for days. He risked his own life and didn't even think twice about it, my dear! One day you'll have to decide what is worth more, the money you make as a lady of easy morals or the warm love of an honest man. You know I care for you either way. But this might be your once-in-a-lifetime chance. Besides, the mine will be a great source of income even if you stay away from the brothels. I'm just speaking the truth, beautiful!"

Lorraine listened to Cotton Joe's speech and tears pooled in her eyes. She knew her trusted friend was right. "I hurt him terribly when I rejected him, Joe."

"Yes, but despite your hurtful behavior he risked his own life to save yours."

"You're right, Joe. I'd be a fool to let that amazing man get away. I'm sorry, but I have to find him now."

Cotton Joe winked at her. "Go ahead, I'm fine here. Got everything I need. Take one of my horses and ride to your man."

Lorraine got up and went to her house. She changed into a riding skirt, and after saddling one of Joe's horses she rode out of town in a hurry. She didn't find Jesse at the mine. It was Sunday, his well-deserved day off. No telling where he was now.

The handsome miner sat in his rocking chair at his home. He missed his friend's presence at the mine. *Man, am I relieved that Cotton Joe will be well enough to join me underground again soon.* Jesse yearned for Lorraine as well but didn't want to think about her too much.

They had hardly seen each other since that night when he shot Wild Linc. The marshal had questioned him about the shooting, but Jesse was declared innocent the very next day. He was a much-respected man in Tombstone now after the news had travelled through all the saloons and brothels that he was the one who had saved Lorraine Bernard's life.

He didn't care about the praise. He had lost the woman he loved, and that was devastating. Jesse hadn't realized how deep his feelings for his boss were until she turned away from him in the middle of the street. *I've fulfilled the task of protecting her so now it's time for me to decide whether to leave town or continue working in the mine.*

Right now, he had no clue what he should do but most likely he would leave. It was too painful to cross her path regularly knowing she would only be his boss, the woman that paid his wage, nothing more … like his wife, perhaps.

The sound of a horse approaching brought him back to reality. He reached for his Colt 45 and waited. His jaw dropped in surprise when he saw Lorraine coming around the curve on horseback. He lowered the gun and waited for her to dismount.

"What brings you out here? Is something wrong with Joe?"

She shook her head. "No, he's doing fine. Actually, he's healing pretty fast and will chase you down the mine shaft pretty soon," she added with a girlish smile.

"So then, what brings you here?"

She had never been to his place before. She looked around at the house and corral, the ramada the horses stood beneath, and the bench under one of the mesquite trees.

"May I?" she asked pointing to the bench. He nodded, and looped her horse's reins to one of the porch poles.

"It's beautiful and peaceful out here," she smiled.

He stood silently and waited, still wondering what her visit was all about.

She turned to face him. "Jesse, I did you wrong, and I came to apologize."

"There's no need to do that. I understand your position in town. No hard feelings. Let's forget about it. I was a fool to think that things would change after that night together. I know I can't offer what certain other men can.

I was married before and couldn't keep up with the high standards of my first wife, and I sure as hell wouldn't be able to give you the kind of life a judge, for example, could. I have no right at all to try to change your life. I understand that pretty well now."

He looked away, the corners of his mouth turned down, his shoulders slumped. The shady lady sitting on the wooden bench was shocked to realize Jesse had given up on her. *What did you expect? This is your own fault.* She cleared her throat from the lump that was building. Then she spoke slowly, carefully, weighing every word. Lorraine knew what she was about to say would be the most important speech of her life. *This is most likely the only chance I have to change the course of destiny for us.*

"Jesse, I know you're not wealthy or a man of high position. I'm aware how you feel about me. I don't have enough words to thank you for saving my life, and I want you to know that I'm not saying what I'm about to say just because I feel obligated or grateful." She paused to gather her thoughts. "When you came into my life, I wasn't ready to settle down, and yes, maybe I felt cornered. I shy away when I get the feeling that someone wants to control me. My family tried to force me into a life I didn't want years ago. I swore to myself I would never allow anybody to lock me in. I thought you would expect me to give up my life as a lady of sin and control me. It's not easy to let down my guard and to put my heart and future into someone else's hands. I am not used to it. To make things worse, I was certain that you were still grieving over the break up with your wife."

She held her breath for a moment, controlling her emotions. He stood perfectly still, waiting, not interrupting her.

When she looked up, he saw she had tears in her eyes

and her cheeks were flushed. When she spoke again, her voice trembled. "This is hard for me, but I have to admit that since you left my bed, I have thought of you every day. Don't misunderstand me. it's not because of the passion we shared. Although I'm not ashamed to say that you aroused me beyond anything I have ever experienced.

"I've never felt so wanted and yet safe and content in anyone's arms. I've never let myself go so completely and have never felt love and caring from anyone like I did from you. I cannot go back to being a soiled dove because the thought of any other man but you touching me is unbearable. It does *not* feel right. I would rather stay alone than feel any other man's hands on my body. I belong to you, Jesse Connor, and beg for your forgiveness. I was so blind not to see how much you care for me. I love you and pray that you still want me as a companion for the rest of your life. Without you I feel incomplete."

Jesse stared at her, speechless, his jaw dropping. He couldn't believe it. *This amazing woman wanted him, a simple hard-working miner? She was the queen of Tombstone's red-light district and was willing to give it all up just for him? Did she really say, she wanted him for the rest of her life?* He couldn't speak. He stood there and stared at her, not capable of summoning a response.

It's too late, she thought. She got up slowly and walked toward the horse waiting at the porch. She could barely see where she was walking, blinded by her tears.

"Lorraine, please don't go. Stay with me!"

His voice was soft and seemed to come from a far distance. She turned and looked at him. He walked over and lifted her off her feet in one strong motion. She was surprised and threw her arms around his neck to steady herself. He carried her to his porch and into his little house.

She looked around a brief moment. It was a surprisingly cute home, warm, cozy and very clean. "Oh Jesse, it is such a welcoming home you have here. I love it."

"Well, I know you are used to a much fancier accommodation."

She shook her head, but then she realized that Jesse most likely had never brought any woman to this place and that he had originally remodeled it for his ex-wife. She felt awkward for a moment and he sensed it. *Am I really supposed to be here?*

"I was a fool to believe it could ever have been a home for Maggie. She never appreciated me or what I achieved anyway. I'm not trying to replace her, my love. Fact is, the marriage was damaged before I left Kansas. I just didn't want to admit it to myself. In all my born days I've never felt the way I feel about you. If this house was ever meant for my wife, then that wife would have to be you."

A tear rolled down her cheek and she kissed him tenderly. He held her tightly in his arms. *Lord, I thank you from the bottom of my heart that this wonderful woman is still alive, and you sent her into my life. Forgive me for questioning your ways and for doubting you, my Heavenly Father.*

This time when they made love, it was different. Although the feverish passion swept them away, every touch was more intense and full of love—a love they no longer had to hide. They took their time and their hearts melted together, becoming one as their bodies united. Later that evening Jesse got down on his knees and asked Lorraine to marry him, and she happily agreed with tears of joy rolling down her cheeks.

CHAPTER TWENTY-FOUR

* * *

A few days later Lorraine went to Judge Taylor's home.

"My precious Lorraine, how glad I am to see you so well." As usual Judge Taylor was delighted to see her, smiling broadly. She knew she would have to hurt him, but there was no way to avoid it.

"My dear, I have to talk to you about my future. I am very grateful that you offered me a decent life by marrying me, and please, don't think that I haven't considered it." A hopeful expression lit up his eyes.

"Nevertheless, I have to admit that I lost my heart to someone, and I cannot ignore the feelings I have for him. I intend to marry that man. I beg for your forgiveness and hope that you will remain my precious friend."

The judge stared at her, his facial expression crumbling into sadness. A tear caught on one of his ash-blonde lashes. At last he spoke.

"Lorraine, you know I love you deeply. It saddens me terribly to lose you. But loving you means I want the very best for you, always. I promised to make you happy, and if letting you go fulfills that oath then that is how it shall be. If you need me, I'll always stand by your side until I take my last breath."

She rushed to him and embraced him. What a genuine gentleman Judge Taylor was.

"Now my belle of the night, may I ask who the lucky devil is who swept your heart away like one of those monsoon storms?"

She told him about Jesse. The judge nodded slowly. "I am not happy that I am not the one chosen, but I admit that Jesse Connor is a very decent choice, my darling. You couldn't have found a better soul in this town, well of course, apart from me and old Cotton Joe!"

Jesse Connor had true grit. He had saved Lorraine's life, and was a hardworking, decent guy. She had chosen wisely, and Judge Taylor had no intention of standing in her way if it was what she truly wanted.

The following day Judge Taylor spoke to Jesse.

"Young man, I want to ensure you I have no hard feelings against you. My priority has always been to make Lorraine happy, so I have to let her go. You are a good man, and I'll always respect you for the fact that you saved her from that ruthless murderer. But be assured, if you should ever mistreat her I'll chase you through the entire territory to bring justice upon you. If I ever discover that you broke her heart, I swear on the Bible you will be sorry for ever being born. You understand me, young man?"

"Yes, Sir! But I can assure you, all I want is to see her happy."

Judge Taylor and Jesse ended their conversation with a hearty handshake. Yes, Taylor really liked that young fellow. Over the years, he had learned to read a man's character. *That Jesse Connor is an honest fellow, he will treat my precious Lorraine with love and respect. Sadly, I still wish she had decided for me,* he thought as he turned away from the handsome prospector.

***

The day of the wedding was bright and sunny. Many had gathered at the small Tombstone church to witness the happy couple getting hitched. They were the talk of the town.

Some of the fallen angels had gathered, too, but remained at the back of the church—whether out of respect or fear of the local pure women, it was hard to say. Many of Lorraine's former johns drowned their sadness about her permanent absence from the brothels in enormous amounts of whiskey. So Lorraine was still a joy to the saloon owners even after her departure.

"Look at them fools. Even when leaving the life as a soiled dove she still ensures me of good business," the owner of the Oriental laughed.

However, Lorraine had agreed to appear at the Birdcage Theatre or Oriental Saloon as a singer from time to time, and Jesse had no problem with that.

The crowd at the church was in a cheerful mood as Jesse stood next to the priest, looking extra handsome in his fine garb for the day. It was easy to see that he was nervous. *Boy, I never thought that someday I would be happy to be divorced. This is indeed the best day of my life.*

Finally, the bells rang, announcing the victory of love throughout the entire town of Tombstone. All heads turned toward the door to see the bride. Lorraine stepped into the church wearing a long, cream-colored Victorian lace dress. Her hair was pinned at the temples and fell in long corkscrew curls down her lean back, emphasizing her slim waist. A few roses had been braided into her thick, soft hair. She looked like a fairy princess.

Cotton Joe walked her down the aisle, his face lit up in a wide grin. A hush went through the congregation as they all stared at how gorgeous the bride looked. Her cheeks were flushed, and a dazzling smile lighted up her entire face. Jesse watched her walk down the aisle with tears glistening in his eyes. When she finally reached him, Cotton Joe put her tiny palm into Jesse's shaking hand and stepped to the first pew.

The priest looked over the gathered crowd.

"My dear brothers and sisters, we have gathered here today to join these two people, Jesse Connor and Lorraine Bernard, in the holy bond of matrimony. No human being shall ever separate what God united."

The love emanating from the bride and the groom was a tangible gift for each person. Each person in the church was deeply touched. Judge Taylor stood next to them as Best Man, smiling warmly. The priest reached the end of the ceremony. "I now pronounce you husband and wife."

That very moment the church door crashed open with a loud bang. Everybody turned around, astounded by the sudden noise. People blinked against the bright sunlight streaming through the open double doors. It took everyone more than a moment to recognize the intruder standing in the blaze of light.

Blonde Mary stood in the doorframe, a shotgun aimed at the bride. When she spoke, her voice was like a hysterical shriek, and her eyes glistened with madness.

"You think you're going to walk away all smiling and happy-ever-after? My man was ripped away from me because of you, Bernard! It should be me standing up there in front of that sin buster together with my Lincoln. You are nothing but a cheap whore, Lorraine Bernard!

You're no better than me or any of the women on Sixth Street. You won't live in happiness! You don't deserve it. I'll see to that."

The guests couldn't believe what they were witnessing, and many expressed their disgust about Blonde Mary's behavior.

"I swear, you won't get a happily married life, Bernard! I curse you! You'll go to hell where you belong to, you hear me? I'll send you there myself."

Blonde Mary yelled into the church and took aim with her shotgun. Lorraine couldn't move, paralyzed with shock at the unexpected intruder, but Jesse reacted swiftly. The loud boom of the rifle ripped through the building, sending people screaming and running for cover.

Jesse jumped in front of his bride, throwing her off balance while shielding her with his own body. Men ran over to Blonde Mary and wrestled the screaming woman to the ground as she struggled to reload the big weapon. She fought and bit at them like a cornered rattler. Blonde Mary had lost her mind after her lover was killed. Three strong men were required to hold her down. "By Heaven, throw that God-forsaken witch into the pokey" one man yelled.

After a scuffle, they were able to drag her to the marshal's office. They locked her in a cell and she remained there screaming about Lorraine, threatening to kill her and Jesse as well. One of the men smacked her in the head with the butt of his Colt, rendering her unconscious.

The turmoil inside the church was still at a fever pitch. People tried to help the newlyweds to their feet. Lorraine's dress was covered in blood but it wasn't hers. She was pale and in shock, but it was Jesse she worried about. Her husband lay on the floor, his shirt soaked in gushing blood. "I am not hurt. I am not hurt! It's Jesse. In the name of God, help my Jesse!" she screamed at the onlookers.

Apparently, her beloved miner had taken the bullet meant for her. For the second time he had saved her life, but this time he paid a high price. Some of her friends carried him to the doctor's house. Doctor Goodfellow cut open his wedding shirt and examined the gunshot. He took his time while the devastated bride wiped the sweat from his forehead. His face felt cool, and she was scared of losing him.

Finally, Doc Goodfellow walked over to his bag, glancing at her. Lorraine waited for him to start the surgery as she knew he had to remove the bullet as fast as possible before he lost more blood. "Doc, why are you taking so long? Take the bullet out of his chest."

Cotton Joe stood next to her. He looked at the doctor and knew it was bad when he saw the doctor's face. Doctor Goodfellow cleared his throat.

"Lorraine, I am so sorry, but there is nothing I can do for him."

"What do you mean? You have to remove the bullet, Doc!"

The doctor shook his head. "I can't. The bullet is too close to the heart. It's deeply buried in his lung. The moment I remove it, the lung will collapse, and he'll bleed or choke to death. Either way he won't make it. God forgive me, but this time there is nothing I can do." The doctor turned and slowly walked out of the room, trying to hide his own tears of frustration.

Why did he leave? He's treated so many gunshot wounds. Why not this one? "Doc, you saved Cotton Joe, I beg you, please come back! Don't let my husband die."

She stared at Jesse stretched out on the table. Cotton Joe couldn't believe it. *Not now, not today when they finally found each other.* Joe carefully touched Lorraine's shoulder and watched her face, feeling helpless.

Finally, the words of Doctor Goodfellow seeped into her consciousness. She would lose him—Jesse would die. She stared at him while tears streamed down her cheeks. Her husband lay still, shot after being married for only a minute. She sank down on her knees, her head resting on her husband's hand while her tears wet the covers. "Jesse, my beloved Jesse. Please, don't leave me. I need you, my husband, I need you!"

Cotton Joe stood on the other side of the bed, watching the blood of his friend soaking through the bandage. He wasn't ashamed of the tears he cried. What a cruel fate. *Was this God's justice? Was this fair play? Why did the bad ones win at the end?*

Jesse opened his eyes and whispered his wife's name. She lifted her face to him. "You sure looked beautiful today, Lorraine Connor. I am the happiest man on earth."

She shook her head. "If not for me you wouldn't have been shot today, Jesse." He shook his head.

"Don't be foolish, if not for you, I would never have found true love. Promise me you'll stick to the mining business, my beautiful angel. The work of a soiled dove is much too dangerous, and I won't be able to protect you anymore. I am so sorry, my love, but I'll have to walk ahead to where we someday shall be united again."

She sobbed as he tried to raise his hand. He touched her cheek, and she held his cold fingers, kissing them tenderly.

His voice was faint now. "Lorraine, say it to me one more time, will you?"

She looked at him and Cotton Joe turned away, helplessly sobbing like a child now.

"I love you, Jesse Connor, my beloved husband!"

He smiled, then whispered, "I'll pass peacefully know-ing I'm loved so deeply and sincerely by my wife. I'll wait for you on the other side, Lorraine Connor. We will see each other again, I promise!"

He smiled and took his last, peaceful breath.

The cry of a lonely coyote drifted in through the open window.

Jesse Connor was dead.

***

The trial of Blonde Mary took place a week later. She sat on the bench in the court room, rocking back and forth in her shackles. Blonde Mary didn't have the mental capacity to follow the trial.

The judge sentenced her to spend the rest of her life behind bars at Yuma Territorial Prison. Most people would have rather seen her die with a noose around her neck but it didn't make any difference to her. Blonde Mary had lost her mind, had gone insane, and the Yuma Prison was known as the "Gateway to Hell."

It was said that Blonde Mary died of tuberculosis at Yuma Prison after being locked up for five years. She was known as Crazy Mary among the other convicts and had spent her days rocking back and forth while babbling endless stories about her lover Wild Linc Duncan, who would come to break her out and marry her.

EPILOGUE

***

Lorraine Bernard kept her oath and never returned to the work of ill fame. She sold her home in town and lived in Jesse's adobe house.

Cotton Joe ran the mine for her, and the former shady lady spent much of her income helping the fallen angels of Toughnut Street and Sixth Street. She provided them with food and medical support and tried to lead them into a better life.

She never allowed another man to take the place of her husband, neither in her heart, nor her bed. She thought of Jesse every day and remained faithful to him, missing him terribly.

Years later, when she was still a very attractive widow in her early forties, she was about to wash the dishes and briefly glanced out the kitchen window. She took in the weathered bench beneath the bushy mesquite tree with its spindly leaves, her favorite spot to read her books.

She couldn't believe her eyes. "Now who the heck would sit on my bench?" A stranger trespassed on her property. Some cowboy sat on the bench and smiled toward the house.

She gaped and almost dropped a plate. She slowly wiped her wet hands on her apron and lifted her six shooter from the holster that hung next to the door before walking onto the front porch. A woman living alone had to be careful. The cowboy didn't move. Who was he and what did he want ?

As she came closer, she saw the boyish smile, and raised her hands to stifle a cry. "Oh my God!" she whispered. She walked to the bench and sat down, unafraid. The cowboy smiled at her.

"Hello, Lorraine Connor. I've come to take you home with me."

She wept but nodded. Her smile lit up her face, dazzling as always. Putting the gun aside, she realized she didn't need it. No, she wasn't scared anymore.

"Hello Jesse, my beloved husband!"

***

Cotton Joe found Lorraine later that day, on the bench under the mesquite tree. She leaned peacefully against its trunk, the most beautiful smile Cotton Joe had ever seen on her face—except maybe on the day of her wedding.

Her friend removed his hat, lowered his face for a moment in silent prayer, and touched her tenderly on her cold cheek, a tear rolling down his wrinkled face. The most amazing woman and best friend he had ever known in his entire life was dead. "Good bye my beautiful angel. I thank you for everything. You were indeed a God-given gift."

Lorraine Bernard-Connor, formerly known as the most beautiful and successful fallen angel of Tombstone's heyday had gone home to be with the love of her life, her husband, the prospector Jesse Connor.

RECOGNITIONS FROM THE AUTHOR

***

I would like to dedicate this book to all the hard-working prospectors, starting with Edward Lawrence Schieffelin, founder of Tombstone and its silver boom, as well as to all the fallen angels that plied their trade in Tombstone during that era. Without them the town of Tombstone wouldn't exist.

Life was hard, especially for the miners and the shady ladies who were an important part of the society of each boomtown.

Some women were forced into prostitution for various reasons, and many selected that path for the safe income it granted.

Tombstone had a large number of "soiled doves." The red-light district spread over six blocks from Toughnut Street to Sixth Street.

The Miners of Tombstone

None of Tombstone's famous gunfights or Wild West history would have occurred if not for a child of German immigrants named Edward Lawrence Schieffelin from

Pennsylvania, who founded the settlement. He was the first man to find silver in the hills surrounding Tombstone.

A rough estimate of the mining production of Tombstone in 1870s dollars suggests $40 million worth of silver was pulled out of the mines. This would be an unbelievable $1.7 billion in today's currency. Schieffelin's first silver vein was over fifty feet long.

Due to successful mining, the population exploded. Within a year Tombstone turned from a tent camp to a town of over seven thousand souls, with some old documents claiming there were more than fifteen thousand inhabitants at some point. Due to the fact that only land owners were officially registered, that is indeed possible.

The mining business turned Schieffelin into a millionaire after he started with only thirty cents in his pocket. He is buried outside the town limits under a rock monument.

Prospecting was a back-breaking job, and included twelve-hour shifts of chiseling with simple tools and loading rock material with nothing but candlelight to work by. Miners earned between three and five dollars per week. They often became ill from lung damage caused by dust underground, and many died of consumption (tuberculosis).

The mining companies grew greedy and dug their shafts too deeply until they hit more and more groundwater. Even additional pumps running twenty-four hours a day, seven days a week, couldn't handle the seven million gallons of water flooding the mining shafts in the end. An earthquake increased the water problem. Some of the shafts were five hundred feet below the surface. Around 1911, mining companies unable to overcome the flooding abandoned their claims around Tombstone, and the town emptied. Nowadays Tombstone's rich history attracts visitors from all over the world. I am proud to own an original 1880s Tombstone Morgan silver dollar, which I treasure, especially since I know the history and events that stand behind that silver.

The Characters in this Book

The characters of Jesse Connor and Cotton Joe are fictional and represent a composite of the miners of Tombstone's history.

Lorraine Bernard

The character of Lorraine Bernard is fictional, but was inspired by Big Nose Kate who successfully plied her trade as a soiled dove. She was a businesswoman who ran her own brothels. Big Nose Kate (original name: Mary Katharine Haroney) was an outstanding woman with real backbone. Her fame is based not only on her on-and-off relationship with Doc Holliday. She was highly educated, fluent in four languages, and stood her ground even when the going got tough.

Blonde Mary (originally spelled Blonde Marie)

She was the first French madam in Tombstone where she successfully ran a brothel for the French syndicate. She was known as an inflexible but smart businesswoman who ran a large, white-painted brothel on Sixth Street. The establishment was known for its rich furnishings.

She wouldn't tolerate drunks or rowdy behavior in her house of ill repute. Therefore, no saloon or bar was allowed in the enterprise she managed. That was highly unusual for this type of business.

Blonde Mary rotated her girls regularly to offer "fresh" entertainment and provided the best food and most comfortable beds. It was the poshest house of ill repute in the entire town. She made sure the wealthy gentlemen visiting her establishment wouldn't become bored with the available ladies of the night.

Not only was Blonde Mary attractive, but she was also highly educated. Some of the most beautiful girls worked for her. Unlike in this book, she was said to have been humble and well-mannered. She managed to save a great deal of money, and she returned to France where she lived in Paris for her retirement.

China Mary

The briefly mentioned Chinese madam called China Mary was a real person in Tombstone. She was the "ruler" of the whole "Hop Town" section of Tombstone.

No Chinese prostitute or any kind of labor provided by the Chinese was available unless approved and hired through China Mary. She had her own police force and was feared, yet highly respected. China Mary held control over all of the opium tents in town. Apart from that, she was known as one of the most generous and helpful characters in Tombstone and strongly believed in a give-and-take philosophy. Her husband owned the famous Can Can Restaurant.

Wild Lincoln Duncan

I was inspired by a Tombstone re-enactor named Lincoln Leavere for the character of Lincoln Duncan. Although he is the "bad guy" in this story, the real Lincoln is a loving father, talented actor, and Western reenactor.

He played Butch Cassidy as well as Jesse Evans in the TV production *Legends and Lies* (Fox News, 2015-2018), appeared in movies such as *The Gundown* (2011), and was a stunt performer in well-known productions such as the *Lone Ranger* (2013).

Doctor Goodfellow

Doctor George Goodfellow (1855-1910) was highly qualified at treating gunshot wounds. He was the first doctor to perform a successful abdominal gunshot surgery in the territory as well as the removal of an enlarged prostate. Doc Goodfellow was a true medical pioneer who performed the first spinal anesthesia and sterile surgery techniques.

He had wide interests, including the study of earthquakes, or interviewing the Apache chief Geronimo. He was known as a champion boxer. He finally achieved fame after he treated gunshot wounds for Virgil and Morgan Earp. Unfortunately, he couldn't save Morgan. But his testimony absolved the Earps of murder charges after the OK Corral gunfight.

He left Tombstone in 1889 and worked in Tucson for a few years. Later he practiced successfully in San Francisco. Ironically, he lost everything in the 1906 San Francisco earthquake and fire. His house in Tombstone still exists, and many of his medical instruments are displayed at the Courthouse Museum in town.

Books and Locations

I gathered a great deal of inspiration from the following books and locations:

Behind the Red Lights (1993) by Ben T. Traywick.

Soiled Doves, Prostitution in the Early West (2003) by Ann Seagraves.

Biggest Little Book/Historical Tombstone Photos (2004) by Bill Roman.

Tombstone's Treasures: Silver Mines and Golden Saloons (2007) by Sherry Monahan.

True West Magazine

Preserved attractions in Tombstone:
  The Courthouse Museum
  The Birdcage Museum
  The Good Enough Mine
  The Oriental Saloon

A LOOK AT: THE UNFORGIVING DAUGHTER

* * *

CAN YOU ALWAYS TRUST THE MEN WHO RIDE BY YOUR SIDE?

Standing by the grave of her murdered father, Sheriff Townsend, Elli swears she will bring justice upon the killers. Unfortunately, the only man who can help her is about to be hung for a crime he did not commit.

Elli must free Armando Phillipe Diaz to defeat the outlaw pack led by the ruthless Texas Logan. A dangerous chase leads to a long-lost treasure and into a deadly trap. Will Elli Townsend survive and be able to fulfill her oath to her father?

"If you like your westerns sprinkled with gunplay, revenge, romance and unlikely allies; this is the book for you." – Rod Timanus

AVAILABLE NOW

ABOUT THE AUTHOR

* * *

AS SOMEONE BORN AND RAISED IN GERMANY, AUTHOR MANUELA SCHNEIDER'S LOVE OF American Native and Western history might be surprising to some. But her fascination with pioneer life, cowboy heroes, and treacherous outlaws have been her constant companion for as long as she can remember.

As a child, Schneider recalls being mesmerized by American TV shows like Gun Smoke, Little House on the Prairie and Bonanza. In her adult years, Schneider fueled her deep interest in the American West by traveling to the U.S.A. and visiting historic sites like Tombstone, Monument Valley, and Kanab, UT. After experiencing the wild beauty of the Southwest first hand, her desire to write stories of love, struggle, and survival in the Wild, Wild West became even stronger.

After leaving a successful career designing motorcycle fashion for the European market, Schneider penned her first Western fiction novel in 2017.

When not researching or penning riveting stories about Western boomtowns and Native American life, Schneider can be found traveling all over the world, enjoying silver jewelry and spur smithing, studying archaeology as a hobby, and writing her own Western travel blog on manuelaschneider.com.